NEW BEGINNINGS

New Beginnings

R W Belew Sr.

Cover design by Bruce Leone
Copyright © 2015 R. W. Belew Sr.
All rights reserved.

ISBN: 1508791244
ISBN 13: 9781508791249
Library of Congress Control Number: 2015903849
CreateSpace Independent Publishing Platform
North Charleston, South Carolina

I'd like to dedicate this work to my wife and daughter, whose support and inspiration respectively made this book possible.

CHAPTER 1

The sun was just beginning to peek over the horizon when Jeff finally arrived at his favorite secluded spot on his favorite secluded beach.

Southern California had many miles of beaches, but most were severely crowded. Jeff preferred a spot on one of the most southern beaches along the coast. If he traveled south any farther, he would need to speak Spanish.

At this spot, Jeff could unwind from the daily grind of working as a political lobbyist. He had affiliations in most political parties and a couple that stretched all the way to the federal government. He had spent ten of his forty years studying the US political system and that of the local California government.

Since Jeff batted for all the political teams, his services were in demand a great deal. Somehow he always managed to convince the right people at the right time to do the right thing, but in recent years his client list had been decreasing because many of those whom he had helped in the past had fallen into disrepute, and his own sense of right and wrong wouldn't allow him to cast his lot with the lesser elements of the government.

While lying in his beach chair, Jeff could feel the morning sun's first rays coming to rest across his shoulders. Jeff had worked almost daily on his slightly muscular and trim physique. Because he was of average height, it would not serve his career very well to become portly or bulbous, like some of the politicians he had to deal with.

Jeff had not taken on any lobbying projects in the past two or three months because he had noticed something. No matter whom he helped to get legislation passed, somebody else would always pass legislation to negate everything he had worked hard to achieve. Even though his efforts thus far had made him very wealthy, the entire course of his career seemed to have no real point. No progress in California or the federal government could ever be made because all levels of government were only concerned about their own petty self-interests. The people who really paid the price were the average citizens.

It was tough for Jeff not to think of work, because he had spent a vast amount of time plotting, planning, and scheming moves and countermoves for his political clients.

At least here on this lonely stretch of beach he could let his mind wander.

The sun had been up for about an hour, and the sky was reasonably clear and bright. Jeff lay there quietly. He was trying to think happy thoughts while listening to the surf going in and out when, a shadow was cast over him. He could feel on his skin that something had blocked the sun's rays, but he figured it was just a passing cloud that would depart momentarily. He didn't even open his eyes under his sunglasses. After the shadow remained for more than a minute, Jeff became curious about what had happened to his sunlight. Still reclined in his beach chair, he took off his glasses, tilted his head back, and looked straight up. He expected to see a passing cloud. Instead he saw the face of a kindly old balding man in his late sixties staring down at him and smiling.

The man said, "Excuse me, kind sir; I wonder if I might ask your assistance."

Not startled easily, Jeff continued to look up at the stranger and said, "Well, I have no objection in helping you, but I would ask you come around in front of me so I don't dislocate my neck during this conversation."

The stranger replied, "Of course, my good fellow. Most certainly."

The stranger walked around to the front of Jeff's chair. As he moved, Jeff noticed his peculiar attire. The stranger's shirt was white with long sleeves that ended in wide cuffs. Over his shirt he wore a brown vest cut to about the waist. His pants looked woolen and stopped at the knee. To complete his look, he wore brown leather riding boots that came to the top of his calf. The stranger's long, gray hair was tightly pulled to the back of his head in a ponytail tied with a length of ribbon. This man did accessorize very well, for he had a leather satchel slung diagonally across his shoulder so that it lay at his side. Every bit of six feet tall, he was very imposing to behold.

The visitor came to stand in front of Jeff, bowed slightly, and said, "Good day to you, sir. I wonder if you might tell me where I am. I seem to have lost my way."

Jeff replied, "This is Imperial Beach."

The old man looked inquisitively at Jeff. "That might be true, sir, but this helps me not. Is there perhaps a city or town that might be at hand?"

"San Diego's about twenty-five miles north of here. It's a pretty big city, and an old fella such as you could probably get lost very easily."

"Is San Diego from whence you came?" the old man said.

Jeff chuckled a little bit and said, "Yes. It is. I've lived there for a long time. Perhaps you could tell me where you're from. Maybe then I can point you in the right direction."

The man declared, "My estate lies in Alexandria, Virginia, and 'tis my wish to return there."

Jeff started laughing aloud—much to the stranger's bewilderment. Jeff got up from his chair, brushed a bit of sand off his lap, and said, "I think I can help you."

He walked over, took a position behind the stranger, put both hands on the old man's shoulders, and pointed him east, where the sun had just risen. "Alexandria, Virginia, is about four thousand miles in that direction. You might want to pack a lunch."

The stranger snapped, "Surely you jest! I was there just this past evening. I know of no means to travel such a great distance in such a brief amount of time!"

Jeff started feeling bad for this old-timer. He seemed genuinely confused about where he was. Not to mention his attire looked a couple centuries out of date. That could land a fellow in serious trouble in California.

Jeff apologized for his ill-timed humor. "Maybe we should start again. My name is Jeff. Jeff Thompson."

The stranger's posture relaxed, and once more he bowed slightly. "My name is George. George Washington.

My formal title was president of these United States and military general. I am, however, retired from both now."

"Please forgive me for saying so, George, but I am going to assume you're playing some kind of joke on me. The only George Washington I know of was one of this country's Founding Fathers, and he died over two hundred years ago. So I guess what I'm saying is, you are looking pretty good for a dead man. I have seen many pictures of George Washington in my travels, though, and you do favor his image."

"Master Jeffrey, although my years are considerably advanced—and in like fashion, so is my countenance—I've never felt more alive than I do at this moment. It would seem there are forces at work here that neither of us understands, but it appears we are both subjected to them," said George.

Jeff smirked. "Check this out." He reached into his waist pack and produced his wallet. After opening it fully, he reached in, pulled out a one-dollar bill, and handed it to George. "Tell me this, George: whose image is on this piece of currency?"

"'Tis I. A remarkable likeness, indeed," affirmed George.

"Please note the year inscribed to the right," added Jeff.

"'Twas minted in 2014? 'Tis unlikely, for the year is truly 1799."

George reached into his satchel and produced a small pouch. He opened it up, retrieved a few coins from its depths, and handed them to Jeff.

After scrutinizing the coins intently for a minute or two, Jeff replied, "These look to be 1799 Draped Bust silver dollars. I've seen these before, mostly in museums or as part of collections. This mystery seems to be growing. Perhaps we can find some answers together. What do you say to that?"

As Jeff handed George back his coins, he accidently dropped a few in the sand. Immediately, Jeff retrieved them and apologized for his clumsiness.

"'Tis good to find a gentleman of kind heart and disposition—unlike the first fellow I spoke to this morning. He became enraged when I introduced myself. During our discourse he made reference to me being a 'no-good shit-for-brains pecker head.' I am uncertain as to the full meaning of his statement, but I believe he was casting disparagements upon me."

Jeff chuckled slightly. "You're right, George. He wasn't being very nice at all. I, on the other hand, try to keep an open mind when I'm confronted with things that don't quite make sense. That's why I can deal with politicians."

Jeff began to gather up his belongings, and as he did so, he continued his conversation with George. "Well, George, I see two possibilities concerning this mystery. You are either a very well-mannered senior citizen who escaped from a psych ward dressed in ancient attire, speaking in a vernacular that hasn't existed for two centuries, and carrying around extremely valuable coins—or you're George Washington, first president of the United States and father of our country, and you have traveled two hundred thirty eight years into the future for reasons unknown. How's that for some deductive reasoning?"

Jeff thought to himself that there was absolutely no way this could be the real George Washington. The very idea seemed crazy, but this man was clearly in need of assistance, and he seemed to have no bizarre or freaky qualities, so Jeff decided to render assistance to the kind stranger and see that the authorities help him out.

"Your logic is sound, Master Jeffery, but by what means shall we discover the truth as to my predicament?" asked George.

Jeff explained to George there were a number of modern ways to definitively identify a person, such as fingerprints, DNA, facial recognition software, and voiceprint identification. George did not understand any of the terms Jeff used, but he was certain he couldn't remain wandering the beach all day.

"Why don't I take you back to my place as my guest?" Jeff said. "We will continue to explore these strange circumstances and see where they lead us. Does that sound reasonable to you?"

George agreed, and the pair began to stroll in the direction of the parking area. About halfway there, they passed a young woman who was stretched out on a blanket on the sand, sunning herself. She was quite fit and wore an extremely small bikini. Jeff noticed his companion blushing in the extreme as they passed.

After a moment, George said in a hushed tone, "What times are these that would allow a woman to lie about nearly naked upon the ground? Although she was quite handsome and lovely to behold, were she from my era, she would no doubt be jailed for her disregard of public decency." George continued, "I recall when I was courting my own personal vision of loveliness, Martha, on one particular occasion I called upon her rather early in the morning, before she had donned her footwear. For the briefest of moments, I beheld her unclothed ankle, which most certainly brought to my mind several carnal thoughts. Additionally, her hair fell in such a way that it looked extremely fetching."

Jeff smirked at his friend. "George, you old horn dog! It sounds to me as if you really knew how to show a lady a good time."

"Master Jeffrey, we are both men of the world. 'Tis true, I did my fair share of courting in my youth, but I can assure you my intentions were most honorable, and I always remained a perfect gentleman," George stated emphatically.

Jeff smiled. "Nowadays we call those kinds of people Boy Scouts. I probably should take this opportunity to say this is definitely not the world you left behind. In modern times, women are mostly treated as equals to men. Slavery has been abolished for a long time, and equality for all men and women of every creed, skin color, or belief system is now the rule of law. In fact, there is a black man doing your old job. I ask you not to freak out if you happen to see something that doesn't quite fit with what you know to be true. Just so you know, the term 'freak out' means to lose control of one's emotions."

The two men entered the parking lot. Jeff had parked at the far end of the lot, near a few other cars and the Port-a-Johns.

George inquired, "What strange carriages are these? I assume they are carriages, for they sit atop wheels, but I see a curious lack of horses, so I am uncertain."

"These are called automobiles or cars," Jeff replied. "These machines can carry passengers great distances with little regard to weather conditions."

George replied, "Indeed!"

Jeff was finding George's behavior and expressions to be truly odd. Only a very gifted actor would be able to stay in character for a long period of time. Because of all of his dealings with politicians, Jeff could easily spot whether someone was being fake in some way, and so far George seemed sincere and genuine in all of his statements.

The two companions reached the car, and Jeff unlocked it remotely. Jeff walked with George to the passenger side and opened the door for him. Before George attempted to get in, he asked Jeff, "Master Jeffrey, do you know a place nearby where one could relieve oneself of bodily fluids discreetly?"

Jeff replied, "Of course. Right over there are a couple of Port-a-Johns. Think of them as portable water closets. Pick an unoccupied one and step inside. I'm certain you can figure out the rest. By the way, you will find a roll of paper in a dispenser inside. Should you dispose of some solid waste, that paper is used for cleansing your backside. Simply use what you need and discard it in the hole. I don't believe they had toilet paper during your era."

Jeff couldn't believe that he had just told an old man how to use a portable toilet, but it was probably important not to destroy this man's illusions before a psychologist could speak to him, so he decided to cater to George's delusion for now.

George walked over to one of the Port-a-Johns and opened the door. He looked dubious about making use of the toilet, and when the overwhelming odor of its sitting in the morning sun had reached him, he and Jeff exchanged a few glances of uncertainty. Then George stepped inside and shut the door. After a few minutes, George stepped out, finished straightening his garb, and rejoined Jeff at the car. Jeff asked, "Well, how'd it go?"

"'Twas hot and vile and smelled of week-old chamber pots. Even though I completed my task, the experience was perfectly dreadful, much the same as what I am accustomed to at my home.."

Jeff helped George get in the passenger side of the car. Once George was seated Jeff buckled him in. Jeff entered the driver's seat and shut the door.

Jeff drove an Italian sports car. It was slung extremely low to the ground and had a wide wheelbase. The car was black with red highlights and bright chrome rims. Jeff really didn't like this car at all because it was hard to get in and out of and very costly to maintain—and the insurance was a killer too. He much preferred to take taxis because most of his business dealings were in metropolitan areas, anyway.

The car was just an attention-getter for the political clients he worked for. Jeff always felt fake when he drove it to government functions, and he hated it.

Not wanting to scare the daylights out of George, Jeff took some time to describe some of the sensations George would experience on this trip to his residence.

Jeff asked, "How far could a horse run in a span of one hour?"

George answered, "Perhaps seven or eight miles."

"This car, at top speed, can travel two hundred miles in one hour," Jeff stated. "When I start the car, you will hear a machine called an engine. It sits behind us and under the hood. It will roar to life, so please don't be afraid. Using the steering wheel and various other controls, I can choose the direction and speed this car travels. The engine has the equivalent power of three hundred horses, so it's safe to say this car was designed to go very fast. In cities and towns and on highways, we have laws that limit the speed we can travel. So be assured we won't be traveling extremely fast all the time."

George asked, "Is it necessary to lash me down to this chair?"

"At the speeds we will be traveling," Jeff explained, "if we got in an accident, these seat belts would keep us inside the car. That would be much safer than getting thrown outside. Do you understand?"

George nodded. Jeff hit the ignition, started the engine, and revved it a couple times. George seemed unaffected, so Jeff put it in gear and started to move very slowly through the nearly empty parking lot. They did a couple laps around the perimeter of the lot. Jeff started and stopped a couple times to acclimatize George to the inside of the car. George seemed to get used to the car and its movements very quickly, so finally they pulled out of the parking lot and headed to the highway to begin their trip.

CHAPTER 2

Traveling on the secondary roads didn't seem to have any effect on George. This type of traffic was mainly starting, stopping, and turning, but when they pulled onto the highway, George's composure seemed to slip a little bit. Traffic was extremely light. For the most part, it was just them on the highway.

Jeff had just achieved sixty miles an hour when George commented, "The speed at which we're traveling is quite astounding. This sensation of velocity seems quite intoxicating."

Jeff responded, "That's why sports cars are very popular with most people. It is a thrill for individuals to travel at great speeds, but with great speed comes great responsibility. Many people have died by driving carelessly or while under the influence of intoxicating beverages. Cars and other vehicles can really help us conduct our lives, but in some instances, they cost us our lives. We have to take much care in their use."

After about twenty minutes of travel, they began to approach San Diego, and traffic started to become heavier. All the different kinds of cars, trucks, and vehicles of every description they passed and interacted with on their journey amazed George.

"Hey, George," Jeff asked, "how is it you ended up on the beach this morning?"

George replied, "Last evening I journeyed to the southernmost perimeter of my estate at Mount Vernon to place marks upon some trees to be removed. I tarried too long, and darkness came upon me. Even though the stars were in view, the blackness of the woods made it difficult to return to my home. I knew the general direction from whence I came and proceeded accordingly. During my struggle to return, I beheld an area of ground that seemed to shimmer with the brightness of a dozen candles. Ribbons of brilliant color stretched up through the parting of the trees to a point in the sky beyond my view. I strode over to the edge of this vision, and after observing for a matter of minutes, the glow increased a thousand fold—so much so I had to shield my eyes lest I lose them to its fiery brilliance. This condition remained only for a matter of moments. Then it departed. When I uncovered my eyes and my vision cleared, I saw darkness still remained, but the terrain had changed completely. Sand covered the ground, and my ears could discern the ocean's roar."

George continued, "A short time hence, the sun began to make its appearance over the horizon, and I could indeed see I was no longer in Virginia. In my search to determine my location, I happened upon a young man waving a strange divining rod across the sand's surface. As I made mention before, he was most surly upon my introduction. I continued wandering until I happened upon you, Master Jeffrey."

Jeff really didn't know what to think. George's story sounded pretty incredible. Jeff had no scientific background at all, and no one he knew had any knowledge of physics or time travel, so if by some strange twist of fate George's story was true, then there would be absolutely no chance to send him back home. He was still pretty certain that George was simply a very charming but confused old man.

Just outside the San Diego city limits, there had been a pretty severe traffic accident. Traffic was backed up for several miles, so Jeff and George had a considerable amount of time to get acquainted. Jeff was amazed at how sharp-witted and intelligent George was. Jeff didn't know too many senior citizens who were even close to having George's mental acuity.

George stated, "I know I have a great deal of history to familiarize myself with. Perhaps you could provide me with some reference material so that I might learn how this country has fared with the passage of time."

"I have an overabundance of material well suited for that," Jeff remarked. "Since it looks as if we'll be here for a little bit longer, I could give you an abbreviated version of the major events between 1800 and today."

George answered, "That would be most helpful."

"Well then, let's get started," Jeff began. "I think I will skip the events of the Revolutionary War simply because you were there to witness them. As I recall, President George Washington died in 1799, so let's start this narrative at 1800. From 1800 to 1900, the United States more than doubled in size from the original thirteen states.

"In 1803 Thomas Jefferson used federal money and debt pardoning to buy the Louisiana Territory from France."

"Thomas was always a very shrewd businessman," George interjected.

"The United States annexed the Oregon Territory," Jeff continued "the area of Texas, and the peninsula of Florida about 1845. The land that is now California, Nevada, Utah, and Arizona all became part of the United States in the latter part of the 1800's. Right now we are in the southernmost part of California. The ocean we're looking at is the Pacific Ocean. Since your home borders the Atlantic Ocean, you're going to have to travel completely across the country to get home."

"'Tis astounding, the rate at which the country expanded. 'Twas my belief many centuries would pass before America would achieve the stature of the nations of old," George said.

Jeff continued. "In 1812 British forces were capturing US citizens at sea and having them work on British naval vessels. As a result, America declared war on Britain, marched to their capital of their province in Canada, and burned it to the ground. Sometime after that, British forces invaded Washington and burned it to the ground. There was really no victory in this particular war."

George added, "The British have traveled the seas with impunity for as long as I can remember. 'Tis a shame the American fleet was not as vast as the English. Our forces would not have needed assistance from France to end the revolution."

"For a long time, tensions had been rising between the states in the northern half of America and those in the southern half," Jeff related. "This was primarily due to the use of slaves as a labor force. The president at the time was Abraham Lincoln. President Lincoln went through a number of his generals to try to win that war, but he didn't achieve a lot of success until he put General Ulysses S. Grant in charge. The Confederate president, Jefferson Davis, enlisted the help of General Robert E. Lee to marshal his forces. By the end of the war, seven hundred fifty thousand American citizens had died. The South was defeated, and the Union survived. In April 1865 John Wilkes Booth assassinated President Lincoln at Ford's Theatre."

"Assassins are the result of all villainy to my way of thinking." George said sincerely "They are cowardly in the extreme, refusing to face their opponents in open combat."

"July twenty-eighth, 1914," Jeff informed him, "Austria-Hungary declared war on Serbia after a Serbian nationalist assassinated their leader, Archduke Ferdinand. Both sides had allied themselves with other nations of the world, and eventually every country on the planet was at war with somebody. Eventually those countries that started the war ran out of resources and soldiers, and in 1918 a number of armistice agreements were signed that brought World War I to an end.

"In 1939 Germany began to aggressively annex its neighboring countries. Soon they allied themselves with Italy and Japan and formed the Axis powers. The United

States, Great Britain, and the rest of the world's countries summoned their industrial might to drive the invaders back. After years of conflict, the Allied powers had driven the invaders back to their homelands. In 1945 Germany and Italy surrendered.

"During the war, the United States engaged in research called the Manhattan Project. They researched and developed a new type of energy and weapon. In August 1945, the United States dropped two atomic bombs on the Japanese cities of Nagasaki and Hiroshima. Japan immediately surrendered and brought World War II to a close."

George inquired, "I know not of this atomic bomb that you speak of; what is it?"

Jeff said, "Imagine setting off a barrel of gun powder, but instead of damage extending a hundred feet, the damage would extend out one hundred miles and could wipe out an entire city."

"My God, man! The loss of life would be unconscionable!" George exclaimed.

"That's why only two were ever used in combat, but testing and development continued for years," Jeff explained. "During the 1900's, America's industry and technology began to advance rapidly. In 1969 we were the first to land people on the moon, and currently we are making strides toward becoming the first to put a person on Mars."

Traffic finally started to move, so the pair of traveling companions was able to enter the city. The grandeur of the many towers in downtown San Diego thoroughly amazed George.

Jeff pulled to the side of the road in front of an ultramodern apartment building. He turned to George.

"OK, George. This is my apartment building. I stopped here to caution you. When I pull into the parking garage, I'll be pulling the car into a private elevator that'll take us and the car up to my private parking space on the same floor as my apartment. Do you remember when I mentioned before about freaking out?"

George replied, "Be of good cheer, Master Jeffrey. I shall remain steadfast in my composure."

With that Jeff pulled around to the side of the building that held the parking garage. He entered the building and drove to the elevator doors. Reaching above his visor, he produced a remote control that activated the elevator doors. Rolling forward slowly, Jeff entered the elevator, and the doors closed behind them. There was a sound of four distinct clunks as the tire restraint devices clamped onto the car's wheels. The elevator then began its trip up to the thirtieth floor. When the doors opened, the tires were released, and Jeff rolled the car forward into his private parking space, which was actually a room in his apartment.

Jeff and George exited the car, and Jeff opened the door to his apartment. He indicated for George to walk through. As they left the parking area, Jeff pushed a big red button on the wall beside the door. The car started to rotate 180 degrees, so Jeff could pull straight out when he wanted to leave again.

Jeff lived in a two-bedroom apartment. There weren't many walls dividing up the living area. Each of the two bedrooms had its own bathing area and was separated from the rest of the apartment. The decor was extremely modern. The kitchen appliances were primarily stainless steel, as were all the fixtures. The white walls were accented by various paintings and pieces of artwork. The floors were white marble with streaks of gray.

It was one of the tallest apartment buildings in San Diego, and Jeff had a grand view from his apartment. Situated at the city's edge, Jeff's western view of the incredible sunsets was more precious than any artwork he possessed.

Jeff and George entered the kitchen from the garage, and the pair sat down at the kitchen table. Jeff said, "You will no doubt find many strange things in here, George. After we get a bite to eat, I'll take you around the apartment and show you all the amenities. We'll get a good night's sleep tonight, and then tomorrow we can begin to unravel this mystery. Is that OK with you?"

George replied, "It sounds like an equitable plan of action. Thank you for your help, Master Jeffrey."

Jeff grinned a little bit. "I think this evening I'll have to introduce you to my favorite suppertime meal. It is a very popular dish known as pizza. There is a multitude of ingredients associated with pizza, so I will get the works on it, and if you find any elements unpalatable, you can simply remove them."

Jeff pulled out his cell phone and dialed the number to his favorite pizza parlor. After placing his order and hanging up, he noticed George looking rather inquisitively at him. It was obvious by his expression that George had never seen a cell phone before.

George asked, "What manner of contrivance is that?"

"It is a means of communication. By pressing a certain number combination, you can talk to an individual with his or her own phone. It allows you to speak from great distances. There's nothing magical about communications technology. This device is a machine, just like a wagon or carriage from your era. It's just a bit more complicated." Jeff added, "When the colonies were settled originally, the citizens had black powder muskets to defend themselves and hunt for food. The Native Americans—or Indians—used spears and arrows for the same purposes. When the Indians saw white people using their muskets, they no doubt thought it was a dreadful kind of magic simply because the Europeans had technology they couldn't understand.

"You're about to discover a great many things, George." George and Jeff continued their conversation until the pizza arrived. Jeff could tell the aroma had a great deal of appeal for George. They both ate their pizza with great delight. Since neither had had any lunch that day, they were both famished.

When they had finished the supper, Jeff took George to the guest room and said, "George, I don't know exactly what forms of hygiene you're accustomed to or what your sleep habits are, so I'll simply describe what I do most evenings and how I start my day. Then you can modify that to suit your own purposes."

George replied, "Very well then."

Jeff started, "The first thing I would do is get a good night's sleep. I believe this bed is very comfortable. All the guests I've had slept very well in it. In here is the bathroom. This is the toilet. It's similar to the Port-a-John you used earlier, except I am certain it smells better. After you're done cleansing your backside with the paper, simply drop it in the water and press down on this little silver handle. It will flush away like this."

Jeff wadded up several pieces of toilet tissue, dropped them into the toilet, and flushed them away.

George exclaimed, "How remarkable this is. Does every home have one of these? Where does it go?"

"In modern times," Jeff said, "every house has indoor plumbing. The waste that gets flushed away goes to a sewage treatment plant that helps break it down and return it to the earth in one form or another.

"This is a sink with hot and cold running water. This side is the cold, and this is the hot."

Jeff turned on the hot water, and in a few moments, steam began to rise out of the sink. Again this convenience amazed George.

Jeff continued his tour. "This is a Jacuzzi bathtub. It contains hot and cold water also. Simply turn the dial to the left. The farther you turn, the hotter the water will get. Turn it back to the right to make it colder. To take a bath, simply pull this little lever up. That plugs the drain and allows the tub to fill. When you're done with your bath, push the lever down, and it will allow the water to drain away. If you want to take a shower, set the water temperature as I've described. Simply turn the knob up, and the shower will turn on. There is soap here and shampoo here to wash your hair. Bath towels and washrags are here."

Jeff walked over to the sink and opened up the medicine cabinet behind the mirror. He described for George the multiple hygiene products there and what they were used for.

"I usually take a shower first thing in the morning," Jeff said. "After I'm done washing, I come over here to the sink and apply my underarm deodorant, take care of whatever shaving needs I have, and brush my hair and teeth. After I finish this hygiene ritual, I get dressed, go out to the kitchen, have some breakfast, go out the door, and start my day. I'll leave you to it. If you run into any problems, just call me. I'll be right down the hall, and I'll do what I can to get you squared away. OK?"

George said, "Thank you, Jeffrey. I'll do my best to manage all this."

"Put your clothes in the hamper there," Jeff said, "and I will see they are laundered. I will lay sweatpants, a T-shirt, and some undergarments on the bed for you while you're showering. They will make very good sleeping clothes for you. Tomorrow we will pick you up some additional clothing to make your stay more comfortable."

CHAPTER 3

Jeff woke up around eight o'clock the following day. As he lay there in bed, George's naïveté concerning modern conveniences still mildly amused him. The bath George had taken last night seemed to go fairly smoothly, except for the application of the shampoo. He was uncertain how much to use and how to apply it. After Jeff shouted some instructions through the door, though, George grasped the concept of how to shampoo one's hair.

George was standing in front of the mirror with a towel around his waist when he called to Jeff again. He entered the bathroom and approached George, whose back was to him. Jeff noticed a multitude of scars and abrasions adorning his back and arms. For an older man, George still seemed to have a great deal of muscle tone, and his overall body fat was minimal. Jeff realized after a moment that most people living in George Washington's era had to do a lot more work for themselves, and consequently, they would have been in better shape than their modern counterparts.

Jeff approached the sink and said to George, "My goodness, George, you have quite a few scars. Were you in a fight of some kind?"

George looked at Jeff through the reflection of the mirror and grinned a little bit. "A revolution is a trifle hazardous and has a tendency to leave marks upon one's person. Should anyone inquire concerning these blemishes, let it be known that they were there upon my birth."

Both men laughed a bit, and Jeff noted this was George's first real attempt at humor. Apparently back in the old days, they liked to laugh, too.

George observed in the mirror that the shampoo had cleaned his hair to such an extent that it seemed fuller and thicker. It even stood up off his head a bit. The top of his head showed traditional male-pattern baldness, but with his hair as fluffy as it was, his head looked reminiscent of a watermelon wearing a hula skirt. No matter what brushing implement Jeff came up with to try to get George's hair to lie flat, there was no way it was going to happen.

"When we get you some new clothes tomorrow, I'll take you to a very good stylist who can take care of this problem." Jeff then asked, "Have you managed to brush your teeth or use the deodorant yet?"

"I am afraid I will have to rely upon your wisdom on those two matters. I know not of what you speak," George said.

Jeff removed the deodorant from the medicine cabinet, took off the safety seal, and said to George, "This is going to be a little bit weird. And just so you know, if you weren't the father of this country, I probably wouldn't do this for you. Please raise your arms above your head as if surrendering."

George did so, and Jeff applied the deodorant in the appropriate fashion. George seemed unaffected by the entire affair, but Jeff was mildly embarrassed. Jeff teased George. "Good Lord, I hope nobody walks in right now. They would most likely think we were gay!"

George replied, "I would beg to differ with you, Master Jeffrey. Trying these new methods of modern hygiene is most exhilarating. Should people ask, I shall tell them explicitly it has made me feel quite gay!"

Jeff's embarrassment wasn't getting any better. "As far as brushing your teeth is concerned, every school kid in the United States believes you have wooden teeth. According to the historical documents I'm aware of, you had a very fine artisan sculpt you some teeth from hippo bones and gold. Is this true?"

"Indeed," George said. "He was the finest craftsman in the land, and I daresay there shall be no other like him again. He toiled unceasingly for over nine months to make certain my teeth fit well and looked becoming to a gentleman of my station."

Jeff was beginning to have some serious concerns about George's story. Everything he had done and said and the few possessions he had would tend to support his claim, but Jeff kept insisting to himself that it simply couldn't be.

"Let's try this, George," Jeff began. "When I step out of the bathroom, take your teeth out, and set them on this towel. Open this bottle, and pour a little bit of the liquid in this glass. Pour the liquid in your mouth and swish it around so it rinses out your entire mouth. Don't swallow it. You'll find that it bubbles a little bit, and it will feel warm and tingly—almost as though you have taken a shot of whiskey. Again, don't swallow it, though. After a minute or two of swishing, spit it into the sink. Wash it down the drain, and after that take some regular tap water, put it in your mouth, and swish it around. After you spit the water into the sink, I think you'll find your mouth will feel much cleaner. In a moment I will bring you a powder called baking soda, and you mix a little bit of it in some water in this glass. Take this brand-new toothbrush, and use the liquid to scrub your teeth very well. After you're done scrubbing with the toothbrush, turn the water on and rinse your teeth off thoroughly. I believe when you put them back in your mouth, you'll find them a little more pleasing and fresh."

Jeff left the bathroom, and George completed his grooming tasks. Just before the pair went to bed, they discussed their itinerary for the next day. It turned out to be quite busy.

Morning came, and Jeff got out of bed. He went to George's door and opened it slightly to see how he was doing. His guest was still sleeping soundly, so Jeff decided not to disturb him. Around this time every morning, Jeff started stirring around the kitchen to prepare his day's first meal. In honor of his houseguest, he thought a traditional American breakfast would be most appropriate.

Bacon, eggs, toast, orange juice, and a side of sausage gravy seemed like a very good stick-to-one's-ribs kind of meal. The breakfast preparations were nearly complete when George meandered from his bedroom yawning and stretching.

"The bed in your guest room is indeed quite comfortable," George stated. "I also noticed the unfavorable scent that usually accompanies my breath at this early hour was absent when I awoke. This brushing of the teeth seems well worth the time and expense. 'Twas the heavenly smell of your breakfast preparations that actually stirred me from my slumber. Many of the aromas that graced my nose are very familiar and welcome to me. Thank you."

Jeff finished dishing up their plates. "You're very welcome, George. I don't often entertain guests, but when I do I like to go all out as far as the meals are concerned."

The two men shared their meal and discussed the best way to complete the itinerary they had put together. They decided the first stop would be the hairstylist. Jeff's hairstylist worked at a salon across town. His name was Thom Delmar. Jeff had been going to him for a number of years, and Thom always seemed very knowledgeable about the best hairstyles and skincare products of the fashion world.

Parking in town was always a roll of the dice, so Jeff decided to simply hire taxis to take them where they needed to go. This would also give George a chance to meet some of the interesting individuals who lived and worked in San Diego.

Jeff told George that what he had worn to bed would be fine to wear on a shopping trip. All George really needed were socks, tennis shoes, and perhaps a flannel shirt. Jeff donned the same kind of clothes, and the shoppers left the apartment. They took a brief elevator trip to the ground floor and out onto the street. After a moment, Jeff hailed a taxicab, and the two men got in the backseat. They were off.

After about fifteen minutes, they arrived at the salon. The pair walked in, and Thom greeted them by shouting, "Jeffrey, Jeffrey, Jeffrey! It is simply fabulous you've come to see me. It seems like three weeks ago you were here. Has it been that long? Say, who's your rather distinguished friend? You haven't started batting for my team, have you?"

Jeff cut off Thom's rant right there. "Simmer down there, Thom. Don't get your undies in a bunch. If you'll take a couple deep breaths, I'll introduce you. This is my friend, George. We met at the beach yesterday morning. He's going to be staying with me for some time, so what I would like is for you to fix him up with an appropriate hairstyle. He's looking for something turn-of-the-century. Not this century but the one before that. The hairdressers George is accustomed to really don't have the flair you do, so let's see what you've got."

Thom was absolutely giddy over the prospect of working on George. It was going to be quite a challenge simply because of the baldness issue. There wasn't a lot of hair to work with—other than the long ponytail portion that hung below George's shoulders.

"Just look at this!" Thom exclaimed. "I have never seen hair as dried out and frizzy as you have here. Georgie, it's a wonder you haven't just burst into flames walking around with this fire hazard. See the end of your ponytail? This is crap! It's dead. There's nothing here for me to work with. It would be easier for me to get the bristles on my broom to relax than try to breathe life back into this hair. So, Georgie, I hate to be the bearer of bad news, but I'm afraid we're going to have to shorten your ponytail somewhat. Maybe to the top of your shoulders. That way you get a fresh crop going, and you'll look absolutely wonderful! As for the rest of it, you know I have some conditioner here that is just to die for. In fact, two days ago when Raule came to see me…"

Thom was on a roll. George sat there quietly with all the patience of Job and let him ramble on for over an hour and a half. Jeff received some looks of uncertainty from George—especially when Thom started to apply skincare products to the top of his head and face. When Thom finished his masterpiece, he took the cape from around George's shoulders, and everyone got to see George's new look in full view.

George looked as if he had just walked off the set of an epic Hollywood film. His skin looked extremely healthy. His hair was considerably shorter but very clean, and it was cleverly shaped around his ears and shoulders.

George approved. "Master Thom, the work you have wrought upon my countenance is simply amazing. Never before has my image been so grand and gentlemanly. You, sir, are a skilled craftsman, and I will most certainly grace your chair with my presence again. Thank you."

Jeff asked George to wait for him outside for a moment while he finished his business with Thom. George complied, and Jeff said, "I knew you were the right guy, ah, person, eh, individual for the job. Please send me a bill for your services."

Thom replied, "I always do. Hey, give Georgie a big squeeze for me."

Jeff replied, "I'll see what I can do. Thanks again."

Jeff exited the building. When he met up with George outside, George put his hand on Jeff's shoulder and said in a hushed tone, "Jeffrey, what manner of man was that? I was uncertain whether he was, in fact, a man or a somewhat homely woman."

Jeff replied, "Thom is gay."

George said rather curiously, "Indeed. I am, however, unaware of any instance where excessive happiness would cause a man to behave so."

Jeff smirked. "In modern times, sometimes it does."

CHAPTER 4

The next stop on their journey was a rather large department store in a mall. Even though this place had a very typical layout for a mall, high-fashion proprietors occupied many of the stores. They saw Giorgio Armani and Saks Fifth Avenue among the retailers there.

The first store they entered sold outdoor apparel. They had a large variety of denim pants and utilitarian shirts expressly made to wear well and look very stylish outdoors.

A salesperson came up to Jeff and said, "Good morning, gentlemen. How can I help you?"

Jeff replied, "I'd like to get my friend here some denim pants, along with some appropriate undergarments and some good-looking shirts, as well."

The salesperson stated, "I believe I have just what you're looking for."

She led them to the undergarments section, which held a variety of plain, simple cotton briefs and boxer shorts. Additionally, there were some that were naughtier in nature.

George briefly viewed the unusual undergarments and exclaimed, "If 'tis your desire for me to wear these unusual trappings, I believe I'll take this opportunity to decline the honor. Should I find myself wearing such a garment, my manhood would most certainly become damaged beyond repair."

Jeff responded, "I'm inclined to agree with you, George. Perhaps this simple pair of boxer shorts would be sufficient."

George stated, "Agreed."

Over the course of the next forty-five minutes, the salesperson had George try on no fewer than a half-dozen different pairs of jeans. The first pair was a bit tight, so George tried some bigger ones. Then they determined that George had no ass, which sometimes happens to older gentlemen. The woman managed to find a couple jeans that had different cuts in the seat. These fit George's backside very well.

Next, the two men went to the shirt area. Jeff found several button-down shirts that he thought looked becoming on George, but George seemed drawn to the flannel section.

George said, "This material feels soft and warm—unlike the woolen garments that have adorned me before. More importantly, there seems to be no itching associated with it."

They obtained shirts of both varieties, and then the two men took their items to the checkout area. Jeff pulled out his debit card and paid for the purchases.

After they left the store, George asked, "By what means of payment did you use to purchase these garments?"

Jeff replied, "It's called a debit card. I keep most of my money in a bank account, and when I use this card to make purchases, money is taken out of my account and sent to the store's bank. This all happens electronically. I'll explain in more detail later about the economics of the United States and how money is transferred."

After a while the two men found their way to the food court. A variety of restaurants lined its perimeter. It included places where one could get Italian food, Mexican food, and a variety of Asian cuisine. The men made their selections and found an unoccupied booth to eat their meals.

George said, "This is quite a bountiful place to dine. Never before have I seen such a wide variety of foreign fare in one place. Many of the state dinners I've attended over the years have been quite lavish, but never as robust as what is represented here."

Jeff smiled at George. "There are food courts similar to this all over the country, but in truth I prefer to fix my meals at home. I find they taste better and are more satisfying because I took the time to make them."

"Master Jeffrey," George spoke, "you might find this interesting. Years ago, Martha and I were guests at a private dinner with a good friend and associate, Benjamin Franklin. I had received an invitation from Benjamin for the pending dinner several days prior. Even though a meal's preparation is traditionally a woman's domain, Benjamin was not betrothed and had grown quite accustomed to preparing sumptuous repasts.

"Benjamin was often seen in the company of various women, who were no doubt extremely taken by his culinary artistry," George said.

Jeff interjected, "No doubt."

George continued, "Lady Margaret Simmons accompanied Benjamin. She was a woman of refinement and distinction, and she was reputed to be a Virginian aristocrat. All evening, Benjamin regaled Martha and me with unusual stories of the unique contrivances he crafted from time to time, and Madam Simmons had many interesting stories concerning her family's affairs with the neighboring communities."

"I'm familiar with some of Ben Franklin's work," Jeff said. "History records him inventing bifocal glasses and lightning rods. He also dispelled many myths about electricity. I always thought that at some point Mr. Franklin had electrocuted himself and had blown all the hair off the top of his head. Every image I've ever seen has depicted him as nearly bald."

George replied, "'Tis true. Benjamin's head was devoid of hair most of his adult life. As for his penchant for inventing things, I have no great understanding of his work with electricity or many other matters he was involved with, but I do know his intelligence was great. He had much enthusiasm for building this country, and he was a very close and dear friend. It has been nine years since he departed this world, and Martha and I still miss the pleasure of his company."

"I'm sorry for your loss, George. Both my parents died when I was a young man, and I had no siblings to keep me company. I've had my dealings with bouts of loneliness. That's why it's important to have good friends who can be with you when you're lonely."

"Truer words were never spoken." George announced, "I will propose a toast to good friends and the company they keep."

With that, George and Jeff raised their cups of soda and tapped them together in the spirit of the toast.

Jeff remarked, "Just so you know what history thinks of your friend Benjamin, check this out."

Jeff produced his wallet again and withdrew a one-hundred-dollar bill. He asked George to view the image on it.

"Astounding!" George exclaimed. "Benjamin's likeness is quite accurate. My heart wells with joy to know Benjamin's legacy has lived on."

After a few moments of silence, Jeff spoke. "I don't want you to think I doubt your personal integrity, but there is still the matter of definitively identifying you. I know the federal government is not going to crack open your sarcophagus at Mount Vernon to retrieve a DNA sample. Plus, should they find out you're a real time traveler, you will no doubt be carted away and subjected to testing for the rest of your days."

Jeff explained that any circumstances the government didn't understand, they deemed a national security risk. They would swoop in and gather up all the people and materials associated with an episode and take them away to a secret bunker for study.

Jeff continued, "It just occurred to me there might be a way to utilize DNA technology to prove—at least to me—who you really are, George. Let's head back to the apartment and put away our purchases, and I'll make a few phone calls to see if I can set something up."

George asked, "What is this DNA technology you speak of?"

"A lot of this explanation you might not understand, but I can assure you it is an extremely accurate means of identification. We have scientists who have devoted their lives to the study of DNA. DNA is an acronym for deoxyribonucleic acid—a substance that acts as a blueprint for all living things. The DNA that makes up your body is different from the DNA that makes up my body. Each person, animal, plant, and microorganism on the planet has unique DNA. Nearly every species on earth has had its DNA patterns cataloged, so if any remains are discovered, they can be identified. Normally," Jeff continued, "we can match up tissue samples found at a crime scene with a body found elsewhere. If we had a sample from your sarcophagus at Mount Vernon, we could take a tissue sample from you and match it up. As I said, though, the federal government won't allow that. What I plan to do, if I can arrange it, is have your teeth tested to see if they are, in fact, made of hippo bone. I know hippo DNA has been cataloged for many years, so if it matches up, then I can say with absolute certainty you are, in fact, George Washington, former president of the United States. After all, nobody in modern times is walking around with hippo bone dentures."

Jeff assured George the technician would only collect the smallest sample, and his teeth would be in no way damaged. George agreed, and both men headed back to the apartment.

CHAPTER 5

Professor Samantha Snyder was finishing her work for the day in her lab when the receptionist brought back the two guests she had been expecting.

Jeff greeted her. "Hello, Sam. You're looking as lovely as ever!"

Some years ago, Jeff had helped Sam get some legislation passed so she could continue her stem-cell research. She was not an unattractive woman. Jeff had considered dating her at one point in the past, but she seemed way too cerebral for Jeff's tastes.

"Thank you, Jeff," Sam responded. "It would appear the years have been kind to you, as well."

"This is my friend George. He has some unique dental work that needs some scrutiny. As I said on the phone, I was hoping you might be able to identify some DNA for us."

"Certainly, Jeff," Sam replied. "Thanks to the funding you helped us get for the stem-cell project, we were able to get a state-of-the-art DNA-screening device. In a matter of minutes, it can process a sample and compare it to the thousands we have cataloged. Where's your sample?"

Jeff looked at George. "If you please."

George took a handkerchief from his back pocket, removed his teeth, and handed them to Sam. She examined them briefly. "OK," she said. "Let's proceed."

She placed the teeth in a plastic tray and put on her medical mask, eye protection, and gloves. She positioned the lower denture so she could see the space on the lower edge of the appliance between the teeth and gum.

She cleansed the area with alcohol to remove any contaminants and drilled three small holes about one-sixteenth of an inch in diameter and a fourth of an inch deep. After using compressed air to blow off the site, she used a small probe to collect bone samples from the bottom of each hole.

She deposited each sample into a small test tube containing a liquid medium and then subjected each to a centrifuge. After that, she placed the samples in a magnetic field that pulled the DNA strands apart from one another. Then Sam placed them in the screening device.

After about ten minutes, the results were ready. Sam said, "The DNA in these bone samples belongs to the phylum Chordata—more commonly known as the hippopotamus."

George glanced at Jeff as if to say, "I told you so."

Jeff asked Sam, "What's the margin of error for this test?"

Sam replied, "Zero. That's why I took three samples. All three came back with the same results, so the findings are completely accurate. I will fill the holes in with a bonding agent, so the only remnants of our test will be three little blue dots."

Sam wondered why an elderly person would make use of these odd dentures. As she repaired them, she said, "These teeth are made with a jeweler's precision. Why did you have them made out of bone rather than a polymer dental material, George?"

Through a series of hand gestures, George let Sam know it was difficult to speak without his teeth.

Jeff chimed in. "George is a bit eccentric. He has been for years. May I ask another favor, Sam?"

"Sure," Sam replied.

"Could you fix George up with an MRI? He's never had one before, and I thought it might be amusing for him."

"Jeff, may I speak privately with you for a moment?" Sam inquired as she finished rinsing off George's teeth and handed them back to him.

After stepping into a side room, Sam said, "You're up to something. Aren't you? Is this one of your politically motivated projects?"

Picking his words carefully, Jeff answered, "I won't try to be deceptive. We've worked together too much in the past for me to be able to get away with anything. There is a back story to George and the things I've asked of you, but until I have my facts straight, I would rather not go into too much detail." Jeff continued, "As an elderly man, George's perceptions are somewhat antiquated. For the moment, I'm trying to acclimatize him to a more modern way of thinking. There's nothing illegal going on here. I just need your help. If something of a more dire circumstance develops, I will certainly let you know. Is that OK?"

Sam considered his words. "OK, but if you get me involved with one of your political shenanigans, you'll be the one who'll need an MRI. Do you understand me?"

"I wouldn't have it any other way," Jeff said.

Jeff and Sam returned to where George was waiting, and Jeff stated, "Sam is going to take an MRI image of your body, George. There's no discomfort involved."

"Master Jeffrey, I am far too modest for such goings-on—especially in the company of the extremely fair Dr. Snyder."

Sam smiled and said, "Thank you for the compliment, George, but please be assured the only part of your anatomy of interest to Jeff and me is under your skin. An MRI machine can take some remarkable images of the inside of your body, and you will not need to remove your clothes at all."

"You have spurred my curiosity, Dr. Snyder. Please proceed," George stated.

Sam giggled at George's choice of words. "Please call me Sam. Titles have a tendency to keep people at a distance."

"Very well, Miss Sam. Shall we be off?"

George held his arm out to Sam like a proper gentleman. Hesitantly, Sam took his arm, and they walked together to the MRI lab with Jeff trailing behind.

Once in the lab, Sam had George remove all the metallic objects from his person and lie down on the table. George's expressions continued to shift between fascination and dubiousness.

Sam cautioned him, "In a moment, the table is going to slide forward and move you inside this tube. A computer voice will instruct you when to hold your breath and when to breathe. Please hold as still as possible while you're in the tube. It will all be over in about three minutes."

"Very well. Proceed," George replied.

George entered the tube, and three minutes later he was finished. Now it was a matter of waiting for the results. Sam called the two men into the control room and brought George's scans up on several monitors. One screen had George's internal organs in view. Another showed his skeleton, and yet another had an image of his brain.

"You've been a busy man, haven't you, George?" Sam said. "Nearly all your extremities show signs of stress fractures that have since healed over. I see the early stages of osteoporosis and a bit of arthritis in your left knee. There is unusual scarring in an area of your lower intestine, and your brain scan shows you have had several concussions over the years. This is the same type of damage our veterans have when they come back from war."

"Armed conflict is indeed traumatic, and one has a tendency to become injured through the course of it," George replied. "'Tis true. Many wounds were wrought upon my person in the heat of battle, and most regrettably so."

Jeff could tell George's eighteenth-century vernacular was piquing Sam's curiosity. He thought it was time to go. Jeff put his hand on Sam's shoulder and thanked her for all her help. Then he kissed her cheek.

George approached Sam and offered his hand. When she placed her hand in his, he bowed slightly and kissed her hand to bid her farewell. "Thank you, Miss Sam, for all your efforts on my behalf. I do hope fortune favors us both and we can renew our acquaintance at some future time."

Sam started to blush as the two men departed. It seemed as though manners and chivalry had won the day.

CHAPTER 6

The White House was the single most secure building on the planet, but there were times late at night when the Secret Service would see brief glimpses of a figure lurking about the hallways and corridors. He was dressed in flannel pajamas, a dark-blue bathrobe, and fuzzy monster slippers. This foreboding character was usually carrying a large mug of hot cocoa and sipping it periodically to try to relax. This was none other than President Darius Saunders.

In this, the second year of his first term, he had been trying to find solutions for the lack of progress in getting Congress to pass budgets, reform taxes, and back his foreign policy, but endless delays had blocked all his efforts. The garbage the representatives attached to his bills to raise their wages and placate special interest groups also slowed everything.

This evening, the president was on his way to the chocolate shop on the ground floor. He had sufficient pull with the proprietor to gain twenty-four-hour access. He encountered several Secret Service members along the way and paused briefly to socialize. He invited them to share in his clandestine cocoa mission, but they declined and cited further duties they needed to attend to.

The commander in chief reached the door to the shop and punched in the access code. The door swung open to reveal a great number of chocolate-oriented displays ready for purchase by the tour groups that frequented the White House.

President Saunders assembled his hot cocoa from his private stock of mix and the hot water dispenser that was always ready for use. He was cleaning up his mess when he turned to see Agent Dirk Marlin of the Department of Homeland Security standing not two feet away from him.

At over six feet tall, Agent Marlin had an imposing demeanor. He had dark, short hair and hazel eyes, and he was well tanned. These attributes and his suit were his trademark features. Many suspects had assumed they could match wills with him and lost.

The President gasped. "Oh! Damn it, Dirk. What have I told you about sneaking up on me like that? I come down here once in a while to get some hot cocoa and relax, and you have me jumping out of my skin!"

"My apologies, Mr. President. I did wait for you to finish making your beverage before I approached," Agent Marlin said.

"Is there some reason you came down here to see me, or are you just practicing your stealth moves?" Saunders inquired.

"Three nights ago, satellite imagery detected an unusual burst of energy located on the California coast just on our side of the Mexican border," Agent Marlin said. "Ground teams were sent in within twenty-four hours, and the initial report states that a high-energy discharge glazed over an area of the beach roughly thirty feet in diameter. We used wavelength filters on the satellite images, and we determined the discharge's origins were from one or more singularities that formed in that location moments before."

"Were there any witnesses to the event?" Saunders asked.

"Our agents arrived just after noon, and there were only two people in the vicinity," Agent Marlin continued, "a beachcomber with a metal detector and a female sunbather. Neither individual witnessed the event, but they both confirm the presence of two more persons. The comber said he ran into a vagrant in strange attire calling himself 'George Washington,' and the sunbather saw the same individual leave the beach with a male beachgoer."

Saunders said, "Well, Agent Marlin, we should make some attempt to find these people and see if they can shed some light on this mystery. Don't you think?"

"We have a description of the vehicle they left in. It was an extremely customized sports car, so we should be able to pick it up shortly," Agent Marlin replied.

"Remember, Agent Marlin, these men aren't fugitives or terrorists. They could just be two people in the wrong place at the wrong time, so don't go overboard in pursuit of them. Do you understand me, Dirk?"

"Yes, sir. I do," the agent replied.

The president turned to retrieve his cup of now-cold cocoa from the counter, and when he turned back, Agent Marlin was gone. President Saunders thought to himself, *I believe it's going to take two cups of cocoa tonight.*

With a cup of cocoa in each hand and a straw protruding from each cup, the commander in chief of the United States slowly made his way back to his residence.

Upon reaching the elevator, the president fumbled slightly while trying to push the button with a cup of hot liquid in each hand, but eventually he just bumped it with his elbow.

When the doors opened, Saunders was surprised to see his wife's dog, Toby, in the elevator by himself. Apparently Toby was skilled at escaping their residence and at operating elevators, as well. Toby was a plotting and devious Chihuahua who was a delight to be around unless one was the president.

This fact was reinforced when Saunders entered the elevator. Toby latched onto one of his monster slippers and began to shake it violently.

The president growled, "Toby, stop that. Hey, cut it out!" As the elevator doors closed, the president shouted, "Toby, I have an air strike with your name on it!"

CHAPTER 7

Dirk Marlin was the type of agent whose peers considered him an extremist. On occasions too numerous to mention, he had used far too many resources in pursuit of his goals, but his superiors tended to look the other way because he did get results.

In one instance, Agent Marlin drove twenty miles with a terrorism suspect tied to the front of his SUV. During the drive, he visited a number of automated car washes and fast-food drive-up windows. Subtlety was not one of his virtues.

The Department of Homeland Security had a number of private aircraft. One was carrying Agent Marlin to San Diego International Airport. During the trip, he phoned two other agents. He had worked with both before, and they shared some of his extremist views. They asked to meet him in the San Diego bureau's office that evening.

After Agent Marlin arrived at the bureau, he sat at a conference table and waited for the first of his associates to arrive.

Agent Dan McFearson entered the room and said, "Marlin, you old dog. I see you're not stakin' out the jacks" (restrooms) "lookin' fer Osama anymore."

Dirk found that Dan's thick Irish brogue was amusing at times, but there were instances where it was difficult to understand what he was saying. Dan was short in stature but had a very stocky, muscular build. He had medium-length red hair and was clean-shaven except for a thick mustache that ran from the area beneath his nose down past the corners of his mouth. It ended at his jaw line. Dan was brought in as the group's muscle.

Dirk greeted him. "I'm sorry to take you away from your interrogation of billy goats, but I'm sure they will still be waiting for you at your bridge when you get back."

"So yer saying I'm a troll, are ye?" Dan spouted, "Well, I got somethin' for ye to troll right here, me fine friend." With that he made a rather lewd gesture near his groin and began to laugh heartily.

Dirk rolled his eyes and smirked a bit. "It's good to see you, too, Dan."

About ten to fifteen minutes had passed when the last of Dirk's associates arrived. His name was Phillip Hancock.

He was the assemblage's information technologist (IT). Although his physical appearance wasn't threatening at all, there wasn't much he couldn't accomplish with a laptop and a modem.

Dan roared, "Well, if it ain't a wee baby bird fell from its nest! Looks as if I beat ye here once again, laddie."

Phil countered, "I hacked your cell phone to get your position. Then I interfaced with the San Diego mainframe and changed all the traffic lights on your route to green to expedite your arrival. You're welcome."

Dirk and Dan exchanged glances of amazement, and when they looked back at Phil, he had a photograph in his hand. Phil slid it across the table to Dirk. "I also took a snapshot of you, Dan, with one of the traffic cams as you approached the building. For the record, picking your nose is a very unsanitary habit."

Sure enough, Dirk was looking at an eight-by-ten glossy of Dan driving his car. His finger was embedded in a nostril, digging for gold.

Phil added, "I won't be shaking your hand anytime soon."

Dan started laughing once again, and Phil took a seat opposite him. Over a year had passed since the three men had worked together. As they sat there exchanging war stories, though, they felt hardly any time had passed at all.

Dan had just finished his story about how he had subdued a terrorist with a shillelagh, a short walking stick that could be used as a club if necessary, when Dirk interjected, "Gentlemen, we have some business to attend to." He continued, "I've given you both the highlights of this operation over the phone, but what I'd like to do now is get a little bit more specific with our assignments. Phil, please go to the mainframe downstairs and start using whatever surveillance is necessary to find our low-profile sports car. It's black with red highlights and shiny chrome rims. Also have the San Diego PD put out an APB on this vehicle. It should contain two males, one older and one younger. For some reason, the description of this car sounds familiar to me, so review my cases for the last five years to see if there was ever a similar car involved. Dan and I are going to the area of beach that was glassed to see if our teams missed anything." Dirk turned to Phil. "Did you bring the piece of equipment I asked for?"

"I did," Phil replied. "I put it in your SUV before I came in the building. To anyone else it will look like a very fancy metal detector, but in fact it can detect metal, wood, liquid, and gas. It can give the user an ultrasound image of an object to a depth of six feet."

"What is the scan radius?" Dirk asked.

"If there is an object within nine feet, the detector will find it," Phil said proudly.

"Well, gentlemen," Dirk concluded, "we know what we have to do. Let's get to it."

As the three men were exiting the room, Dirk said, "Wait a minute. My SUV was locked up, and the alarm was activated."

Phil replied, "You're right. It was."

Phil beamed with pride as he turned to go start his assignment.

CHAPTER 8

The confirmation that his friend was actually the historical George Washington surprised Jeff. The matter of what George was to do now that he was here was still foremost on Jeff's mind. George was a senior citizen, so there were really no job prospects available. Perhaps he could use George as a political consultant for any upcoming projects.

During the morning's meal, Jeff said, "Tell me, George, how would you choose to proceed from this point? Your identity is as you said it was, and that for me was the mystery to be solved. What sort of life do you want to build for yourself?"

"I know not," George replied. "My uncertainty is great in this future time. Every person should have a purpose for being, lest he become slothful and indigent. 'Tis true I have come to rely on you a great deal, Master Jeffrey, but I have no wish to take advantage of your kindness and hospitality.

The ability to make my own way in this world is much more desirable."

"The rest of the world still doesn't know about your existence, and I believe that if it does come to light, your safety and welfare could be in serious jeopardy," Jeff continued. "I suggest we find the means to give you a new identity, and hopefully you'll be able to live out the rest of your days in peace."

"I am not at all comfortable with the prospect of living a life of covert existence," George confessed. "The specters of fear and dread would be ever present, and my quality of life would suffer on unspeakable levels. At some point I will have to navigate this city and time on my own."

"How about this, George? I'll take you on as a political consultant. That way you can work in a field you have a lot of experience in. It would give you that purpose you spoke about, a jingle for your pocket, and some action for your pride. There is a small apartment below mine you could reside in. It isn't as grandiose as mine, but it would be a good place to start, and I would be close at hand should you need any assistance."

"It does indeed sound equitable," George replied. "But as to my identity, I would prefer to keep my original name. 'Twas given to me with love by my parents. Thus to part with it would grieve me beyond measure."

"Very well then, George," Jeff said. "I will do what I can to honor your request."

"You stated once before you had an abundance of reference material through which I could read," George recalled.

"Yes," Jeff replied. "I do have some here, but when I need to do serious research, I look online or go to the public library across town."

"I know nothing of this 'online' you speak of, but I am familiar with libraries, so perhaps a journey is in order," George said.

"We shall go there directly," Jeff affirmed.

The library was in a rather shabby part of town. Slum-like areas surrounded the location, and gang insignias were scrawled everywhere. Jeff didn't feel comfortable leaving his car parked on the street, but cabs didn't generally go to that part of town.

The two men entered the library and sought out the head librarian.

She was in her late sixties and had her gray hair pulled tight up into a bun. Her face had wrinkles. Her overall appearance was prim, proper, and extremely Victorian.

Jeff had spent a lot of time there over the years, so he had gotten to know the librarian very well. Although it was generally accepted she was surly and cold, Jeff knew she had an unspoken soft spot for him—most likely from the kindness of his demeanor.

When they reached the main desk, they found her engrossed in cataloging new books. Jeff got her attention by saying, "What a piece of work is a man! How noble in reason, how infinite in faculty! In form and moving how express and admirable! In action how like an angel! In apprehension how like a god!"

Without looking up, she stated, "Quoting Shakespeare does not relieve you of the responsibility of returning the four books you checked out three months ago or paying the fee to the tune of fourteen dollars and seventy-three cents, Mr. Thompson."

Jeff and George exchanged glances, and Jeff said, "George, I'd like you to meet Mrs. Clara Witherspoon, the head librarian and reluctant friend of mine. Mrs. Witherspoon, this is my good friend and business partner, George Washington."

Mrs. Witherspoon stated, "I have no time for your nonsense, Mr. Thompson, and I ask that you return the books immediately."

George interjected, "Madam, I can assure you Master Jeffrey has stated my name correctly. I understand your confusion with my historical namesake. However, George

Washington is my name, and I would thank you to honor it, as I will always honor yours."

Mrs. Witherspoon stood from where she had been sitting and walked to the counter opposite George and Jeff. She gave George a momentary glancing over. "I am dubious your name is truly George Washington, especially since Mr. Thompson is involved. Be that as it may, you appear to have manners and decorum, so I will take you at your word, Mr. Washington, and I will trust this isn't some puerile joke."

"Mrs. Witherspoon, I thank you for your leap of faith, but I find it curious you should have a mild disdain for Master Jeffery. How could this be?" George inquired.

"Some years ago, Mr. Thompson was engaged in some kind of political horseplay, and I wound up being interrogated at length by the Department of Homeland Security. It was a perfectly dreadful situation that I want never to repeat," Mrs. Witherspoon emphatically stated.

"Would you have any objection at all if I remained to use some of your reference materials? I give you my word they shall not leave the premises," George stated.

"I have no objection, Mr. Washington, but I ask Mr. Thompson to go retrieve the overdue books and pay the subsequent fine."

George agreed and walked with Jeff to the door. "Mrs. Witherspoon seems singularly minded that you return those books she mentioned," George remarked.

Jeff asked, "Are you going to be OK here by yourself? I'm probably going to be gone for over an hour."

"Master Jeffery," George stated, "I have fought in a revolution. Should my safety be the focus of your concern? I shall be fine, and should I be in need of a good right arm to come to my aid, I have no doubt Mrs. Witherspoon will charge in to defend me."

"It is silly of me to worry, isn't it?" Jeff said.

George replied, "Indeed."

With that, Jeff left to get the overdue books, and George, with Mrs. Witherspoon's help, set about catching up on two hundred years of history.

CHAPTER 9

Dirk and Dan arrived at the site and found the tide had washed away the bulk of the glazed-over sand. The pair took turns running the detector over the sand's surface, but they only recovered some pop cans.

Dirk decided to scan the area between the beach site and the parking area. Slowly, they walked toward the parking lot and waved the detector in wide arcs along the ground.

At one point they uncovered a stash of opened contraceptive wrappers. Dan commented, "Looks as though there's been a wee bit of shaggin' going on here, boy. My willy could not take that kind of use and still be attached to ma' body!"

Dirk kept scanning, and over the course of two hours, they managed to collect six dollars in change. They scanned their way to the parking lot and found nothing significant.

Dan sat in the front of Dirk's SUV, took the change he'd collected from his pocket, and emptied it into an old coffee cup.

As Dan was rifling through his cup of change, he said, "Well, Dirk, this morning cannot be a waste of time. We got enough here to stop off and get us a pint or two. Know any good pubs?"

Dirk shook his head with disappointment, and Dan chuckled at him. Something he saw in the cup interrupted Dan's mirth. It looked like a quarter, but it was a bit bigger than the rest. Dan fished it out of the cup and exclaimed, "Hello, me beauty. What do we have here? Looks like a vintage coin of some kind, but it looks recently minted. Not a scratch to be had on it, for sure."

Dan handed it to Dirk, who examined it closely. His partner was correct. It did look freshly minted. If this coin had been in the sand for any period of time, abrasions would have covered it. Dirk held it out at arm's length, snapped a picture of it with his phone, and placed a call to Phil.

Phil answered, "What's up, Dirk?" Marlin heard a snicker on the other end.

"I'm sending you a picture of a coin. I need to know everything about it. You copy?" declared Dirk.

"Dirk, we're on cell phones. There's no need for radio jargon here. It's quite confusing. I have your picture and will get you the information shortly."

"Do you have any info on the suspect car?" Dirk asked.

"Yes, I do, as a matter of fact," Phil said. "About four years ago, you investigated illegal campaign funding among groups of lobbyists. One of the independent lobbyists you questioned was—"

"Jeffrey Thompson!" Dirk said, "Who happens to drive a unique sports car. That little smartass lobbyist still pisses me off after all this time."

"In case you're interested," Phil continued, "your fancy sports car is currently headed to the downtown area via Main Street. I'm uploading his current address and any current information about him to your vehicle's navigation system. I'll slow him down a bit so you can arrive before him."

"Very well then, Phil. Thank you for the update."

Dirk was about to hang up when Phil added, "Oh, FYI, the air pressure in your passenger rear tire is four pounds low; you're thirty-five miles past your oil change; the automatic light timers in your house are not set to daylight saving time; and your bank account is out of balance by fourteen cents. Just saying."

"We're going to have to have a little talk, aren't we, Phil?" Dirk responded.

"Yes, we are," Phil countered. "Fourteen cents could cause a lot of problems."

When Dirk ended the call, Dan said, "I think this year I'm gonna have the little pain in the arse do me taxes."

Dirk began to wonder why all three of them seemed to work so well together, considering they all got on each other's nerves.

Dirk found working with Dan irritating at times because he had no inner monologue. Anything he thought came spilling out no matter what the situation was, and it usually contained a sexual innuendo or some disparagement. When he would address his superiors at the Department of Homeland Security, he would magically gain a vocabulary and be extremely proper, but it no doubt stretched the ability of his vocabulary.

Dan was born in the United States like most agents, but his parents had immigrated to the States some years before. They had instilled a sense of Irish pride in him that some folk found obnoxious and irritating.

Although he didn't carry it all the time, Dan would sometimes carry a shillelagh. He toted a gun like all agents, but there were times when gunfire caused more problems than it solved. Plus, he was one to enjoy a good knock-down-and-drag-out fight.

Phillip Hancock was simply the nosiest person on the planet, a show-off, and an insufferable know-it-all. His remarkable computer skills allowed him access to everyone's digital life, but as far as anyone knew, his intrusions into one's personal life were more jovial than mean spirited. Dirk had cautioned him that one day he would get a taste of his own medicine and regret his intrusions in a major way.

Phil flaunted his wealth of knowledge in the faces of the people he spied on, so he made a number of enemies over the years.

CHAPTER 10

Dirk and Dan arrived at the front garage door of Jeff's apartment a few minutes before Jeff. The agents concealed themselves in some darkened corners and awaited Jeff. The elevator doors opened, and as Jeff's car emerged and entered the apartment, the agents slipped inside the garage as well. Jeff walked several paces to his kitchen door. He was about to enter when Dirk stepped into the light.

"Mr. Thompson," Dirk said, "It's been quite some time since we last spoke."

Without turning, Jeff responded, "Not nearly long enough, Agent Marlin."

Dirk asked, "How'd you know it was me?"

"I didn't at first, but then I recalled that when I stepped out of my car, I caught the distinct aroma of Guinness and sweat socks. I realized there was a leprechaun nearby, and I knew you wouldn't be too far away."

At that point Dan stepped from his hiding place. "I'll wager three pints this leprechaun can ruin yer day, Mr. Thompson."

"No doubt," Jeff remarked. "If you two gentlemen would join me in my apartment, I will see what I can do to make your visit as brief as possible. I'm fairly certain I have a pot of gold lying about here somewhere."

Dan was still grumbling when Jeff motioned for them to take seats at the kitchen table. The agents sat down, and Dirk tried to start his line of questioning. Jeff moved to the fridge to get a beverage and held up a finger to request that Dirk pause for a moment. Dan watched Jeff carefully as he chose his drink, set it down on the table, moved to a cabinet in the living room, and opened the door to retrieve something.

"Don't you be gettin' cute with yer hands there, Thompson. I'm watchin' you!" Dan exclaimed.

Jeff slowly removed an air horn commonly used in boats, and he donned a pair of noise-reducing earmuffs. Then he showed the horn to Dan.

Dan said, "What are you fixin' to do with that, laddie?"

"This!"

Jeff squeezed the trigger, and an earsplitting screech shot from the horn. The two agents quickly covered their ears. The blast only lasted a couple seconds, and then Jeff put the horn and earmuffs away.

Dirk uncovered his ears. "What the hell was that for?"

Jeff tilted his head up slightly and started scanning the area. "I know you're out there, Agent Hancock. You might as well pipe up and join this conversation."

Over Jeff's stereo and PC speakers, the men heard, "Damn it, Thompson! My ears are killing me!"

Jeff sat down at the table across from the agents and proclaimed, "Now we're all here; what's on your minds, fellas?"

Even though Dirk was irritated beyond measure, he began to question Jeff. "There was an incident on Imperial Beach a week ago. A witness saw you there. Did you see anything unusual?"

Jeff replied, "No. I do sometimes go to that beach for some early morning sun and surf. What happened?"

"I'm sorry, Mr. Thompson. That's classified," Dirk stated.

Why am I not surprised? Jeff thought. "It's going to be kind of tough to answer your questions if I don't know what it was I was supposed to have seen," Jeff said.

"I'll lead this investigation, Mr. Thompson. Now, our witness said you left with somebody. Who was it?" asked Dirk.

"He is my friend and business partner, George Washington."

Jeff knew Agent Marlin would never believe him, so he needed to come up with a plausible history for George. He only had seconds to create it. Jeff had gotten good at thinking on his feet. This skill had come in handy over the years, and dealing with politicians had honed it to a fine edge.

"You've got to be kidding me," Dirk fumed. "I'm trying to ask serious questions, and you're being a smartass."

"Agent Marlin," Jeff explained, "I am aware George's name is uncommon, and I had a bout of disbelief when I first met him, as well. I have found George insightful about this country's politics and extraordinarily kind. He is helping me work on a new campaign idea, and that's why I took him on as a business partner. I'm sure if you come back later this evening, he would be happy to answer any questions you have."

"Then he lives here?" Dirk asked.

Jeff answered, "Yes, he does."

Phil chimed in. "Dirk, I'm detecting strong vocal stress patterns from Mr. Thompson. This suggests deception."

Jeff hollered, "It couldn't be you've invaded my privacy once again and subjected me to a cryptic line of questioning. Oh, no. It couldn't be that!" Jeff thought carefully for a moment. "Agent Marlin, I saw nothing out of the ordinary at the beach on the morning in question. I am reasonably sure George didn't, either. If you want to ask him directly, then return about nine o'clock. You may pose your questions then. Also please bring Agent Hancock with you. I'm allergic to virtual presences."

"I suggest you keep this appointment, Mr. Thompson. Missing it would be extremely bad," Dirk cautioned.

"With Agent Hancock monitoring my every move and being under the munchkin of death's watchful eye, I don't see how I could miss it."

"OK. Nine o'clock it is, then," Dirk confirmed.

After both agents left, Jeff went around his entire apartment and unplugged all the electronic devices Agent Hancock might use to spy. He gathered up the books Mrs. Witherspoon had requested and headed back to the library by cab. It seemed to Jeff his car might be too conspicuous under current conditions.

CHAPTER 11

Before leaving the apartment, Jeff turned off his cell phone and then went down to the lobby. He used the landline to call a friend who drove a taxi there in San Diego. His name was Franklin; like some celebrities, he had no last name. He was originally from Jamaica. He and Jeff had become friends over the years, and he had been instrumental in helping Jeff dodge some surveillance he had experienced the last time he had dealings with the Department of Homeland Security. With Franklin's dark skin and dreadlocks, he was the perfect companion to have when visiting the less desirable areas of San Diego.

When Franklin picked up the line, Jeff asked that he pick him up at the library around noon. Franklin confirmed the appointment, and Jeff hung up and hailed a regular cab to take to the library.

After Jeff entered the library, he found George deeply engrossed in some historical material. He had stacks of books piled up all around him.

Jeff took a seat beside George. "I'm back, George," he said quietly. "How's it going?"

"It would seem this country has had quite a colorful history," George replied. "I am still sorting through the nineteenth century. Your absence was considerably longer than an hour. Did you misplace your books?"

"No. It's much worse," Jeff confessed. "I had a visit from the Department of Homeland Security, and they know of your presence. We need to come up with a place to hide you."

George asked, "What, precisely, are they aware of?"

"They asked me if I saw anything unusual at the beach the morning we met. The people we saw told them we were there." Jeff continued, "I told them you are my business partner and you are residing with me, but they still want to talk to you. They are expecting us back at my apartment at nine o'clock. That should give us enough time to get you to a safe place."

"Master Jeffery," George started, "'tis your desire for us to live in fear and slink about for the rest of our days?

There might be a time more covert travels become necessary, but at this moment, we are not criminals. We have broken no laws. Perhaps answering their inquiries will satiate their curiosity. We need only answer those questions they ask directly."

Jeff countered, "If they find out you're the real George Washington, they will take you away."

"Jeffery, do you still doubt my abilities to deal with problems and protect myself?" George asked.

"I am understandably concerned," Jeff said.

"Fear not," George continued. "We shall be victorious this day and on the morrow celebrate fully our spoils!"

"I think you're being overly confident, George, but I will respect your wishes and let you state your case," Jeff conceded.

About that time, Mrs. Witherspoon approached Jeff. "Mr. Thompson, I see you've returned. Do you have the overdue books?"

"Yes," Jeff replied. "I returned them to your assistant and paid the fine when I first got here."

"I trust, Mr. Thompson, you will be more prompt in the future."

"Yes, Mrs. Witherspoon. Thank you for your understanding," Jeff retorted.

Mrs. Witherspoon rolled her eyes at Jeff's remark and then said to George, "Mr. Washington, were you able to find a sufficient amount of historical material?"

"I did indeed, Mrs. Witherspoon. Thank you for your efforts on my behalf," George answered.

"Not at all," Mrs. Witherspoon replied. "I enjoy your company unlike your associate." She turned and walked away.

Jeff leaned toward George and in a hushed tone said, "I think she's in love with me."

"Methinks not," George replied.

With about fifteen minutes until the cab was set to show up, Jeff and George sat on the front steps of the library and discussed a strategy for dealing with the agents. Off in the distance came a weak cry for help. The sound seemed to come from a narrow alley across the street, and it caught their attention.

The two men entered the alley at a brisk jog. Trash and junk of every description littered the passage. Tires, old furniture, and broken toys lay among the mess. George and Jeff navigated around the obstacles to find a young woman and what looked like three gang members accosting her.

Concealing themselves behind a Dumpster, Jeff asked, "Well, George, how would someone of your era handle three gang members assaulting a woman?"

George looked around the mess and spotted a broken child's bicycle. It had what used to be a flag on the back of it. The fiberglass rod that used to bear a flag was about three and a half feet long and had a small brass ball on the tip. No doubt the ball was a safety measure for kids.

George grabbed the rod at the base and pulled it from the bicycle frame. He turned to Jeff and said, "Thusly!"

George approached the trio stealthily until he reached striking distance. Then he stepped into view and assumed a fencing posture. "Gentlemen, this young woman appears to be enjoying herself not. Perhaps you would be so kind as to release her."

The three men stared at George. They were somewhat confused for a moment, and then they began to laugh loudly. Their mirth subsided. The smallest of the group was wearing a bandana across his forehead, and his pants were hanging off his butt. He stepped toward George.

George held his ground, and the youth exclaimed, "Look, old man, you bein' all up in my business is gonna get you whacked. So you best be gettin' on down the road!"

George stated, "You, sir, are ill mannered and poorly dressed. Unless you desire a trouncing the likes of which only God has viewed before, unhand that woman and depart posthaste!"

"Man, I got somethin' for you to depart!" the assailant yelled.

The young man reached behind his back and produced a gun, but as he brought it to bear on George, the makeshift sword he had crafted was already being wheeled in a very high arc. George brought the small brass ball crashing down on the gangster's hand, and he dropped the gun immediately. With one deft move and a change of position, George lunged forward and poked the criminal in the eye. He turned away from George and bent at the waist. George brought the whole of the rod across his buttocks three times in rapid succession, and this left the young man lying on the ground and holding his face and butt.

The entire skirmish lasted only a couple seconds. The other two gangsters dropped the girl and rushed to defend their comrade. As the first man approached, George simply sidestepped him. As the man passed, George struck a glancing blow across his buttocks, as well. The man crumpled to his knees, and he held his butt with both hands. The third man launched himself through the air in an attempt to tackle George, but George bent at the waist and spun around. The man passed overhead to land on his stomach on the pavement.

By the time the third assailant had gotten to his feet, George was already there with yet another thrust to the eyeball. This rendered the man unable to continue.

The stinging effects of George's weapon had diminished, and the second criminal rejoined the fight. The man charged George. At the last moment, George swung the weapon in an elegant arc up from the ground. It caught the man under the chin with the little brass ball and blasted his jaw. The swing lifted his feet high into the air, and he landed flat on his back.

All three men were on the ground, unable to move.

George walked to where the second man had landed and placed the tip of his sword on the man's eye. "I have bested you gentlemen in the extreme," George said. "Do you yield, or should I continue?"

All three men spoke in a jumbled chorus that they were done. George walked over to where the young woman was lying. He bent down and held out his hand. She reached up and took it, and George helped her to her feet. There wasn't much left of her shirt, so George removed his flannel shirt and draped it across her shoulders.

"Are you injured, miss?" George asked.

The woman said, "I'm just a little banged up. If you hadn't been here, these assholes would've screwed me for sure. I am so grateful you helped me. Most folks around here don't want to get involved."

"Do you require any further assistance?" asked George.

"No. I only live a block or two away," the woman said.

"Please keep the garment. I hope the rest of your day isn't as troublesome as it has been thus far."

The woman turned and started walking away. Then she turned back. "By the way, what's your name, mister?"

"I am George Washington," George said proudly. The woman looked rather dubiously at George, and then George said, "I know 'tis a rather odd name, but 'tis in fact what I am called."

"I guess it doesn't really matter," the woman confessed. "To me you will always be G. Dub. Thank you."

With that statement, the woman departed. George returned to where Jeff was standing agape.

As George approached, he whipped his new weapon through the air several times. "This device could be quite handy at some future time. Do you think the owner would try to reclaim it at some point?"

"It was among a pile of junk, George. I don't think you have anything to worry about." Jeff paused. "That was the most amazing thing I've ever seen, George. How did you learn to do that? I don't even think you broke a sweat."

"What a pitiful state of affairs 'tis when passing ruffians can accost young women at will," George replied. "One has to defend oneself if survival is the goal. These ill mannered youths were in desperate need of a trouncing and a lesson in decorum. Perhaps they will reconsider their actions before attempting such a deed again."

The three gang members started to limp and drag themselves away in the most pitiful retreat imaginable.

"I have no doubt about that. I hope you don't think me a coward, George, for not helping, but you seemed to have the situation well in hand," Jeff said.

"Be of good cheer, Jeffery. I know if I were in serious peril, you would have come to my aid," George concluded.

"I think our ride is here," Jeff said. "Let's go, G. Dub."

"What does that mean, Jeffrey?" George asked.

"It is a slang acronym for your initials. It's meant as a term of endearment."

George replied, "Indeed."

CHAPTER 12

The two men arrived at the cab that was waiting for them at the library. Franklin's cab was yellow like all the other cabs, but as Jeff and George approached, the appropriate doors opened automatically. Jeff took the seat beside Franklin, and George sat in the backseat. In front of both men were small compartments with glass doors that contained cold beverages, and just above them were small video screens showing news and sports channels.

Franklin greeted Jeff. "How are you doin' this fine day? This part of town ain't for the lighter persuasion. You know what I mean, mon?"

"You're right, Franklin," Jeff replied. "Sometimes you've got to live on the edge, though. You know what I mean, man? Take us to my apartment, please."

"Yeah. That's for sure. You sayin' the homeland boys be makin' troubles for you again?" Franklin inquired.

"Yes. As a matter of fact, it's the same three agents who gave me so much grief last time," Jeff answered. "Now they're not only watching me but also my new business partner and friend…uh…um…G. Dub."

George looked at Jeff as if to say, "What are you talking about?" Jeff returned a look that told George to go with it for now.

George stammered, "Yes. I am…uh…G. Dub. 'Tis a genuine pleasure to make your acquaintance, Mr. Franklin."

"Please just call me Franklin, mon."

"Very well, Franklin. I will honor your wishes," George conceded.

"So, Jeff, you got the hit mon, the nerd, and the pixie trailin' after you, then? How you gonna play this one out?"

"G. Dub and I have an appointment to speak with them later tonight," Jeff answered. "Hopefully we can settle whatever the matter is quickly. However, it would be prudent to have some untraceable transportation available if necessary."

"I'm hearin' you on FM, mon," Franklin said. "I'll have the gettin' the hell out of town posse ready to roll when you say so."

"You know, Franklin," Jeff said, "you're probably still on their radar from the last time you had dealings with them.

I'm certain Agent McFearson still hasn't forgiven you for parking your cab on his foot so I could get away."

"Oh, the little sprite just had his feelin's bruised a bit. He did look funny hobblin' about with that Irish walkin' stick and a cast on his foot, though." Franklin laughed loudly.

"Nevertheless," Jeff continued, "our discussion tonight needs to leave them feeling as though I am simply working on a campaign and G. Dub here is harmless."

The men were halfway back to the apartment when George commented to Jeff, "Although my studies of this country's history are far from complete, I've noticed that at times of great strife and uncertainty, this nation's citizens turn to national leaders and heroes to find comfort and continuity for their lives. In recent periodicals and publications, I have become aware of growing unrest within all castes of citizens regarding a very broad range of subjects. 'Twas the conflicting governmental legislation that took root that started these dark times."

As the cab neared the apartment building, an idea came to Jeff like a breath of fresh air. They needed a campaign of patriotism to remind the citizens who they were and what it meant to be American.

The cab pulled over in front of the building, and Jeff gave Franklin his final instructions. Then the two men exited the cab. Jeff always felt safe when out and about with Franklin because of his understanding of San Diego's lesser elements, and he knew he could count on Franklin to be there when needed.

CHAPTER 13

Upon entering the apartment, both men retrieved beverages from the fridge and found seats on the sectional couch to relax. There were several hours to go before the appointment, so they had plenty of time to prepare.

"There are only two things I'd like you to do," Jeff said. "First, be yourself. When asked questions, tell the truth about what you know to be certain. Second, any questions pertaining to your activities beyond when we met on the beach, I'd like you to talk around. Give them as little information as you can short of lying. They have ways of determining if a person is telling the truth."

"I believe I can do that quite well, Jeffery," George replied.

"OK. I'm going to go to the diner across the street and use their landline to make a few phone calls. I'll be right back."

George asked, "Would you perhaps have any tools and material suitable to fashion a proper hilt and grip for my new sidearm?"

"There are many tools in the chests in the garage and various pieces of wood and plastic under the bench. Help yourself. I'll be back shortly," answered Jeff.

George entered the garage and found the tool chests. Some were for working on cars, some were for electronics, and others contained various kinds of carpentry hand tools. Under the bench he found pieces of wood from a broken chair, some rubber tubing, and some broken kitchen appliances.

After some deliberation, George discovered an aluminum funnel from an old juicer. He forced this to fit over the handle end of the fiberglass rod. He slid it up high enough that about six inches of the rod protruded from the funnel's bell side. Next, he found a rather ornate spindle from the broken chair. It had a reinforcement rod running through its center. George pulled the metal rod out and cut the spindle down with a handsaw to match the fiberglass rod's length. The hole in the center of the spindle was too small to slide over the shaft, so George found a variety of files and used one of the round ones to enlarge the spindle hole enough to get a good friction fit when he slid the new handle onto the end of the fiberglass rod. With a little bit of coaxing, the handle slid all the way up to the inside of the aluminum funnel. This completed the project.

George was admiring his handiwork when he heard what sounded like the front door opening. Jeff had only been gone for about twenty minutes, so George doubted he was returning.

George went to the door leading into the kitchen and shut off the lights in the garage. Then he took a position in the shadow of the open door and waited to see what would happen.

After a few minutes of silence, George saw the silhouette of a pistol starting to protrude into the garage. As George had done before, he swung his weapon in a high arc and brought the little brass ball crashing into the wrist bone of the intruder. The gun flew across the darkened garage. The unknown person yelled and sprawled backward into the kitchen.

From the sound of voices, George could tell there were at least two people in the kitchen. George quickly moved to the far side of Jeff's car and lay down on his stomach with the rear tires directly between him and the door.

George peeked around the front of the tire, and he could see the former gun carrier's partner attending to him. After a few minutes, the second interloper turned his attention to the garage. The stranger turned on the garage lights and then looked under the car to see whether anyone was crouched on the other side.

George stayed behind the tire. He lay perfectly still until he saw a hint of an ankle at the back of the car. With all the strength he could muster, he swung his weapon laterally about six inches off the floor and caught the gunman right in the lower shin. A mighty yell went out, and the stranger dropped to his knees. George rapidly swung again. This time the weapon was about twelve inches off the ground, and it blasted the gunman squarely in the groin. A high-pitched scream echoed through the garage, and the man landed on his face. George sent two more lashes across the floor to land directly on top of the intruder's head.

Realizing the man in the garage was out of commission, George rolled to the right and looked around the front of the tire. He saw the first gunman still sitting with his back against the wall in the kitchen, desperately trying to get his wrist to work.

George quickly found a length of wire nearby and tied the unconscious man's hands and feet to each other over his back. He grabbed another wire and cautiously walked to the open kitchen door. He poked his head out briefly to check the hallway in both directions, and it appeared as though there were only the two of them.

George walked directly up to the man with the broken wrist, put the little brass ball in the middle of the assailants' forehead, and said, "Do you yield, sir, or shall I continue?"

The man had no power of speech left in him. He just sat there and vibrated like a jackhammer. George grasped him by the front of his shirt and lifted him to his feet. Then he sat him down in a kitchen chair and used the wire to tie his elbows together around the back of the chair. George tried to spare his wrist any more trauma.

Jeff returned to his home to find Agent Hancock with a broken wrist and tied to a kitchen chair. Agent McFearson was tied up like a fatted calf and laid unconscious on his living room floor.

Jeff's composure slipped, and it took a few moments before he could articulate what was on his mind.

George could tell Jeff was in distress, and he calmly said, "When we first met, you advised me not to 'freak out,' as you so eloquently put it. I might advise the same for you at this time."

Jeff took a couple deep, cleansing breaths and asked desperately, "Is this man dead?" He pointed to Agent McFearson.

"No. He is still among the living," George replied. "Although it might be appropriate at this juncture to find medical attention for both these gentlemen."

Jeff began additional deep, cleansing breaths when he began to sputter and gag. "What the hell is that smell?"

George replied, "I believe you will be in need of a new kitchen chair."

Jeff didn't know whether to laugh or cry. Seeing these agents debilitated was funny as hell, but this incident was going to complicate things greatly.

Jeff summoned the police and an ambulance, and he and George gave their statements to the officers. Jeff also supplied a copy of a surveillance tape of the entire incident to the police and hid the original elsewhere.

The police and medical personnel were finishing up when Agent Marlin arrived. He entered the kitchen, where he read the police report and the statements George and Jeff had made.

Agent Marlin got Jeff's attention and asked to speak with him briefly in the garage. George was curiously absent, but Jeff complied and joined Agent Marlin in the garage.

The two men stood at the back of Jeff's car, and Agent Marlin started the conversation, "Agent Hancock is still in shock with a broken wrist. Agent McFearson has a bruised shin, a ruptured scrotum, and a concussion. Can you think of any reason I shouldn't take my gun out and shoot you in the head right now?"

"Well, Agent Marlin, you could do so if that's what you truly want to do, but you would certainly run the risk of pissing George right the hell off—at which point you would most likely end up like your associates."

Dirk started to laugh wickedly as he slowly reached for his weapon. He had only completed half the maneuver when he felt the coolness of a small brass ball resting on the back of his head.

A very polite voice said, "I've grown quite fond of Master Jeffery during the time I have spent in his company. I would be dismayed if any bad circumstances were forced upon him or if harm befell his person. In fact, I would most certainly have to respond in an ungentlemanly manner."

Without turning around, Dirk said, "You must be the George Washington I've heard so much about."

"Indeed, Agent Marlin," George replied. "I do regret meeting you under these circumstances. 'Tis most unfortunate. I would have much preferred to speak with you directly at the appointed and agreed hour, but seemingly you have been gifted with subterfuge and deception."

"Not very many people get away with calling me a liar," Dirk said.

"'Tis certainly an odd statement you make," George said, "considering they would be speaking the truth. I would still be willing to speak with you in a public forum if that would help dispel whatever the issue is you have with me."

"We are way beyond diplomacy now, old man."

"Then you and I are in disagreement, and I believe 'tis time for you to depart."

Jeff's cell phone suddenly rang. After looking at the display to see the incoming number, he handed it to Dirk. "It's for you," Jeff said.

As Dirk answered the call, George removed his weapon from the back of Agent Marlin's head. "Hello…um…Mr. President," Dirk stammered. "I…but there are two agents down, and…yes, sir. I'll be there in a few hours."

Dirk handed the phone back to Jeff. "Thank you, Mr. President," Jeff said. "I will e-mail the videos of the raid by the two other agents and this encounter with Agent Marlin shortly. Thank you again. Good-bye."

Dirk turned to face George for the first time. "It looks as if you got your wish, Mr. Washington. I'll be leaving now. The president wants to see me. Just know this is not over."

"Indeed. 'Tis not, Agent Marlin," agreed George.

Then Dirk walked past George and left.

Jeff said to George, "One of the calls I made was to a member of congress who owed me a favor. He put me in touch with the director of the Department of Homeland

Security. After I described the circumstances of the raid, the director said to hand the phone to Agent Marlin when my phone rang if he was here. I think it worked out very well."

CHAPTER 14

President Saunders sat at his desk in the Oval Office. The first item on his itinerary today was the debriefing of Agent Dirk Marlin.

Before Dirk entered the room, the president had all the chairs removed so Agent Marlin would have to stand the entire time. Sometimes a little discomfort could aid in getting to the truth.

President Saunders sent for Dirk, and after a few moments, one of his aides escorted him to the front of the desk.

"Agent Marlin," the president began, "when last we spoke here in the White House, what were my instructions?"

"You asked me to investigate the energy anomaly on the California coast and interview all the witnesses," Dirk replied.

"That's right. This was a fact-finding mission," President Saunders stated. "From what I've gathered from the director of the Department of Homeland Security and the videos supplied by Mr. Thompson, you engaged in unwarranted surveillance of a lobbyist known for his honesty in the political arena and an elderly business partner. Agents Hancock and McFearson bypassed Mr. Thompson's apartment security with guns drawn, and an old man with a bicycle flagpole handed their asses to them. In less than five minutes, both your agents were incapacitated. Is this the sum total of this incident, Agent Marlin?"

"Yes, Mr. President. It is," Dirk replied.

"From what I've been told, you have had dealings with Mr. Thompson before," Saunders continued. "After crawling up his ass with a microscope for six months at the expense of a million dollars, you found he was totally compliant with all lobbying criteria. Is this true?"

"Yes, Mr. President," Dirk responded.

"Then I can only assume you have some personal issue with Mr. Thompson, and for reasons only known to you, he seems to be the target for your aggression. You will share those reasons with me right now," the president stated.

"Mr. President," Dirk began, "with all due respect, I was unaware you had taken over control of the Department of Homeland Security and necessitated me reporting to you. When we initially spoke in the White House, I reported to you at the behest of the director, and now I find myself doing it yet again."

"Agent Marlin," the president continued, "after nine-eleven, the Department of Homeland Security and the Patriot Act were shoved down the throats of the American people. In the years since, agents such as yourself have gone too far in their investigations. They have brought condemnation on the Department of Homeland Security and every administration since. I want the American people to be on our side and willing to supply us with information readily. You had an appointment to sit down and talk with both these individuals. Why did you choose instead to try to take them into custody? I could have used my authority as a club to usurp the chief's position and assert myself, but after a lengthy discussion with him, it was determined we feel the same on this matter. If the chief felt any of his agents were jeopardizing the integrity of the Department of Homeland Security or this administration, he could ask for a presidential review. Together we would find a way to deal with these threats."

"Do you consider me a threat, Mr. President?" Dirk asked.

"Agent Marlin, of what value is spending a vast amount of time and money tracking down terrorists before they cause problems if this country's citizens end up hating our guts?" Saunders demanded. "Your record thus far has been one of overzealous aggression, and I'm questioning if you have the right temperament for this job. It appears you detain and cause grief to suspects not because of what you're investigating and not because what you're doing is legal and proper, but because you can. From my perspective, you appear to be a mean spirited individual with an ounce of authority who enjoys wielding it far too much.

"I want you to take some time off. Take a good, hard look at yourself, and consider if this is the best career move for you. There are many other governmental agencies that could use a man with your experience. If in the end you decide to stay, your presidential review will be at an end, and the chief will have a new assignment for you. To be absolutely clear, you are to stay away from Mr. Thompson and his associate. The violation of this order will carry the harshest reprimand. Do you understand me, Agent Marlin?"

"Yes, Mr. President. I understand completely," Dirk responded.

"Then report to the chief for his debriefing, and enjoy your time off. That is all, Agent Marlin. The best of luck to you."

Dirk simply said, "Thank you, Mr. President."

Then he turned and left the room.

CHAPTER 15

The morning after all the commotion, Jeff and George sat across the breakfast table from one another. Neither said anything for the longest time while they ate, and then Jeff started to snicker. At first he was very quiet, but as he gained volume, it caught George's attention.

George asked, "Is there some portion of recent events worthy of such mirth?"

"The sight of two agents totally disarmed and the look on Agent Marlin's face when you got the drop on him in the garage are images I'll never forget," Jeff said. "After all the problems they have caused me personally, on our first go-around and now this, it feels good they should find themselves in trouble."

"Tell me, Jeffery, of all the people present during that unfortunate conflict, who would you say was the most frightened?" asked George.

"That's easy. Agent Hancock. I have the kitchen chair to prove it," answered Jeff.

"In truth, Jeffery, I suffered the most fear during the encounter," George admitted.

"How can you say that, George? I've seen you fight on two occasions. Each time, you tore through the bad guys like a whirlwind," Jeff stated.

"'Tis true. I fought well, and the brass ball on the end of my weapon did make a very satisfying thump as it collided with my assailants," George acknowledged. "Nevertheless, Jeffery, I have killed so many in my lifetime. I can scarcely close my eyes without seeing apparitions of their faces looming closely.

"I have consoled myself with the knowledge they were all foreign soldiers purloining our freedom and liberty, but there are times when even that thought gives me little comfort," George added remorsefully. "As for this conflict, I had no knowledge of the assailants' true identities until after the fact. I have always believed in discretion first, and I was uncertain of their true purpose, so I merely disabled them. Should they have continued their attacks against me or someone I thought well of, I would have surely dispatched them with great haste. The act of killing is certainly never easy, even when one's life hangs in the balance. But I can say with absolute certainty that sometimes 'tis necessary," George said.

"I have never killed anyone," Jeff said. "I can't even imagine what you deal with daily, George. I think it would be safe to assume the period of history you're from was more about personal survival than my society. From what I know of historical accounts and from what I've witnessed personally, I know your heart is a good one, and I think you should find great comfort in that."

"Thank you, Jeffery, for your kind words. My soul does feel a trifle lighter," George said gratefully.

Jeff and George had finished their breakfast, but the overall mood in the apartment was still pretty heavy. Jeff asked George to follow him into the garage and to bring his sidearm with him.

Both were standing in front of the workbench when Jeff said, "I think I have a few ideas that will help both of us out. I'll have a project I care about to work on, and you'll have a new purpose to immerse yourself into. Sidearm's and swords are objects of extreme beauty, so in that spirit, I have a few things here you can use to enhance your weapon's looks and functionality. Here are a number of polishes to increase the brilliance of the metallic surfaces. Here is one for fiberglass, and these are extremely sharp carving knives for doing detailed woodwork. It occurred to me many great weapons of the past usually carried names, so while you're detailing your sidearm, you can consider a suitable name. What do you think, George?"

"You, sir, are correct," George stated. "There are refinements to be wrought upon my sword. Thank you, Jeffery, for this splendid idea, and I would ask one further thing of you. If you would be so kind as to find me some leather hides and appropriate tools, I should like to make a scabbard for my instrument of justice."

"OK, George. I believe I know just where to go. I'll be gone for a few hours, so I'll see you here at lunchtime."

Jeff gathered a few items and put them in a briefcase. Then he entered his car and departed.

George pulled a stool from under the workbench, sat down, and began polishing the sword's hilt. Even though it had started out as an aluminum funnel, it was beginning to take on a lot of brilliance. It shone brightly under the incandescent light. The fiberglass rod polished up equally well, and the crown jewel of the instrument was the brass ball on the end. George spent a considerable amount of time rubbing and buffing this item, and when he was done, it shone like a beacon in the night. When George passed it through the air quickly, a discernible trail of light emanated from it.

Even though the grip was a chair spindle, George was able to carve a fairly intricate pattern into the wood that allowed for a much better grip during combat.

Jeff returned some time later, and as he entered the apartment, he began to move cautiously, peer around corners, and advance stealthily.

He poked his head into the living room and saw George was nowhere to be found. He walked quietly down the hallway and looked into George's room. He suddenly felt the coolness of a small metal object at the base of his skull.

"You know, Jeffery, a man's room is his place of security," George whispered and snickered.

Jeff turned around slowly. "The last time I left you alone, you ended up detaining a couple people. I was concerned it was the start of a pattern."

"Be of good cheer, Jeffery," George said. "That is a matter I should like to discuss with you at length, but first I ask for your thoughts on my side arm's appearance."

He handed Jeff the weapon, and Jeff studied it intently for a few moments. "George!" he exclaimed. "You've turned what were essentially bits of junk into a piece of artwork. This is marvelous."

"Thank you, Jeffery," George said graciously. "Your kind words fill my heart with joy."

The two men retired to the living room and Jeff noticed a pensive look on Georges' face, and Jeff said, "What's on your mind, George?"

"The two agents who assaulted me. What are their fates?" asked George.

"I believe they're still recovering at the county hospital. Why do you ask?" Jeff replied.

"Agent Marlin has declared the right of vengeance upon me. He strikes me as a fellow of insurmountable determination, and we will no doubt host his presence once again.

"I should like to speak to the other agents," George continued, "to dissuade them from similar courses of action. The first step in communicating is to gain the person's attention. I believe I have theirs."

Jeff agreed. "Of that I have no doubt. OK. Let's take a trip. Hopefully these agents are in agreeable moods. By the way, have you picked out a name for your weapon?"

"Indeed," George stated proudly. "In our last conversation, I referred to it as my instrument of justice. Using that as a premise, I have decided to name my sword Iustitia. 'Tis the Latin form of 'justice.'"

"Is there any formal ritual for naming a sword?" Jeff asked.

"Not that I'm aware of," George replied. "A simple declaration will suffice."

CHAPTER 16

Jeff and George were standing by the nurses' station when Police Chief Adams arrived. Jeff had called him to chaperone their visit. That way no further laws would be broken.

Jeff had known Chief Adams for a long time. The chief was in his early sixties, a couple years away from retirement. Jeff could tell that after he introduced George to the chief, George had found a kindred spirit. Both men were advanced in years and somewhat war-weary. They shared a similar build, but the chief still had all his hair.

After about fifteen minutes of swapping war stories, George asked, "What condition are these men in, Chief Adams?"

"Well," the chief began, "Agent Hancock has a broken wrist, and the doctor says it'll heal just fine. However, he's suffering from some mental stress issues, and the psychiatrist can't even get him to talk."

George said, "If you will allow me to speak to him, I believe I can help."

The chief agreed, and George entered the room quietly. He sat down in the chair beside the agent's bed. Agent Hancock still seemed catatonic and didn't even acknowledge George's presence. He just continued to stare off into the distance.

George sat there and watched him for ten minutes or more. Then he calmly said, "I know your fear. I have seen what you have seen and felt what you have felt. You saw your death and were powerless to overcome it."

A number of tears started to travel down the agent's face.

"Fear me not, Agent Hancock," George continued. "I am not a demonic apparition sent to harm you. I am but a man who was as fearful as you during our encounter. Please turn your gaze upon me and know the truth."

The agent only responded with more tears. George reached forward with his hand and placed his fingers on the side of the agent's jaw. George slowly turned the agent's head to face him. "My name is George. What's yours?"

The agent's jaw started to gape like a fish out of water as he tried to speak. After much effort, the name "Phil" came from his lips.

"Greetings, Phil. I am honored to properly make your acquaintance." George removed his hand, and Phil continued to look at him. "I am certain at this moment your mind is ablaze with thoughts and images swirling about in a pool of chaos." George paused. "I ask you to concentrate on me. Listen to my voice, and perhaps together we can sort out the madness." George paused again. "'Twas your first time in a battle?" asked George.

"Yes," Phil uttered slowly.

"What has befallen you is the epiphany of your own mortality. Mortality and I have been traveling companions for a great many years. I have been thrust into the heat of battle, and in every instance, mortality has been there staring me in the face. After a while, I found it to be a great source of strength. Knowing my days were, in fact, numbered, I resolved that as long as I pursued my heart's desires fully, my death would be a gracious one. As yours will be one day, too."

Phil still was having problems speaking, but he managed to say, "You have been there."

"I have indeed. Should you find your heart's true calling, I believe the rest will attend to itself. No one can tell you what you want. Not me, and certainly not Agent Marlin. If you wish to discuss this further, I know a person with your resources can find me. Get well soon, Phil," George concluded.

Phil whispered, "Good-bye."

George left the room and rejoined Chief Adams and Jeff. Upon his arrival, the chief asked, "How'd it go?"

"I did speak with Phil briefly. He is currently engaged in a battle on the field of his mind. I believe I gave him enough ammunition to be victorious, but, Chief Adams, I would ask you to use whatever means at your disposal to keep Agent Marlin away from Phil. At least for a while. Phil has enough demons to battle currently." George continued, "Now, let us attend to the other agent."

As the trio walked to Agent McFearson's room, the chief cautioned George, "This next guy is pretty foul tempered, George. The medical staff had to sedate him twice after he initially regained consciousness. Maybe I should go in there with you."

George simply said, "This entire affair seems centered on me, Chief Adams. 'Tis most likely I will be the one to resolve it."

When George entered the room, he saw Agent McFearson dozing, so he took a seat at the foot of the bed. A nurse came in after a few minutes to check on the agent's IV, and in doing so she disturbed McFearson's slumber. After she left, the patient saw George sitting there.

"Who in the hell are you?" McFearson snapped.

George replied calmly, "I am unfortunately the one who placed you here. My name is George Washington."

An instant flash of anger crossed the agent's face. He made a pitiful attempt to rise from the bed, but the combination of drugs and concussion prevented it.

"Please calm yourself. The battle is over, and you have been victorious," George said rapidly.

Every word Dan spoke caused him discomfort, but that wasn't going to prevent him from speaking his mind. "What are you sayin', ya blatherskite? You're sittin' over there, and I'm fair jacked to the hilt in this bed. I ain't feelin' victorious at all," the agent exclaimed.

"You're speaking in terms of physical damage. 'Tis your *mission* that brought you to my residence that I refer to. In that, you have prevailed," stated George.

"Are you daft, man? I was to take you into custody for questioning, and now I'm in here with a bum leg, my manhood briste' (*splattered*) all over the front of me, and a headache to the tune of a case of Guinness. How do you figure I won?" Dan asked.

George quietly said, "I am sitting here and not running loose in society. I have no immediate plans to leave. If you have queries to pose, now would be an excellent time, but before you begin I would ask, what is your first name, Agent McFearson?"

"It be Dan, laddie, and don't you be forgettin' it, 'cause sure as you were born, we'll be seein' each other again," Dan threatened.

"Since you broached the subject," George continued, "Agent Marlin seems set on harming me in some fashion. I was curious about your thoughts on the matter."

"Do you expect me not to put a hurtin' on you, after what you done to me?" Dan asked.

"I would ask you to consider something before you go through the time and trouble to end my days," George said carefully. "What would you have done if armed strangers had forced entry into your home? Would you have subjected them to a series of questions, losing the advantage of surprise, or would you have found a means to disable them and secure your residence once again?"

Dan's frustration grew for a moment as the validity of George's point sank in. Then the anger subsided altogether. "Aye, Mr. Washington. You do make a wee bit of sense."

"Thank you, Dan, for this ounce of concession. Please address me as George. I am reasonably certain that statement was extremely hard to make. I propose this—you and Agent Hancock allow the doctors to mend your wounds. Upon your recovery, come find me wherever I happen to be, and we can discuss these matters further. If your pride is still aflame, and if the only means to quench it is combat with me, then so be it. If you choose combat, I would ask you to bring Agent Marlin. Perhaps his pride can be quenched, as well."

Dan agreed to his terms, and as George prepared to exit the room, Dan said, "George, not once during your visit did you poke fun at me size or heritage. That has not happened for a long time. Why not?"

"There is a time for jesting, Dan," George stated, "and I don't believe that now is the time. If you should choose not to combat, I would be honored to share in some well-mannered frivolity with you and trade embellished war stories. Get well soon, Dan."

With that, George left the room.

CHAPTER 17

Several weeks went by after George visited the agents in the hospital. The director of the Department of Homeland Security was so embarrassed by the entire incident that he contacted George through Jeff and apologized for his agents' manners.

George expressed concern about any future dealings with errant agents and asked permission to contact the director directly should the need arise. "My respect for you and for what your agency has been tasked with is great," George stated. "Nonetheless, on two separate occasions, your office has interrupted Mr. Thompson's life, and now it would seem I have been drawn into the fray. If the need should arise and I require your direct intervention, I ask for permission to contact you for guidance on the matter."

George's logic was inescapable, so the director consented, and the episode seemed to be at an end.

George used his time to continue studying at the library. Mrs. Witherspoon quite often became the topic of conversation between Jeff and George. It seemed as though the librarian had taken a liking to George. Apparently George's manners and charm had inadvertently tugged on her heartstrings, and George didn't seem to mind.

Jeff was true to his word, and he secured a small apartment just below his own for George to reside in. Any worries about George's ability to take care of himself had long since been dispelled. Jeff also purchased a cell phone for George. It was very simple in design, and after a period of time, George became quite good at using it.

The stipend Jeff granted George for his consultation activities was sufficient to allow George a comfortable standard of living. George still had reservations about the use of credit and debit cards, but he was able to function well enough on a cash basis.

Jeff asked at one point if George had considered getting a driver's license and a car. George replied, "'Tis a grand thing to be able to travel about so. However, at times I feel my age upon me. I would be dismayed if I inadvertently injured someone through my unfamiliarity with motor vehicles and the laws governing their use. Besides, I find Mr. Franklin an engaging character, and he is willing to convey me to any destination I choose."

Jeff saw his point and let the subject drop. The first few days George spent in his apartment were quiet. Jeff dropped in from time to time to check up on him, and it was at these times George missed Martha most. It was true Mrs. Witherspoon had caught his eye, but Martha still had the majority of his heart.

There wasn't much Jeff could do except listen, but it did seem to help George a lot. Jeff encouraged George to find other people he had met since his arrival to spend time with and build some friendships with. However, the true nature of his origins would have to be suppressed.

George contacted Police Chief Adams, and he began periodically to socialize with him when the chief was off duty. Chief Adams was a widower who also had time on his hands, so they found some activities to engage in once or twice a week.

When George completed his work on the scabbard for Iustitia, he wore his sidearm proudly. However, when the chief saw George with it, he reminded George it was illegal for citizens to carry sidearm's of any kind in public.

Chief Adams saw the disappointment in George's eyes, so he said, "Tell you what, George. Why don't you and Mr. Thompson join me down at the station tomorrow about noon? Bring your sidearm with you. I think I might be able to help."

George agreed, and the next day he and Jeff arrived at the station. An officer greeted them and escorted them to a briefing room where a dozen officers had lined up in two columns. Chief Adams stood at the far end. Jeff was asked to stay at the beginning of the column, and George was escorted to the front to stand before the chief.

A march played softly in the background, and the chief began to speak. "Mr. George Washington, after reviewing the reports of your conduct during the homeland security case, and after speaking with Mr. Thompson at length concerning your rescue of a woman being assaulted in an alleyway, it is my honor to bestow upon you the honorary title of law enforcement officer and all the rights and privileges thereto."

Chief Adams stepped forward and pinned a shield to the front of George's shirt. "George, may I see your sidearm, please?" George handed it to him, and the chief continued. "What is your weapon's name?"

George replied, "'Tis called Iustitia. It is Latin for 'justice.'"

"Please kneel," Chief Adams asked, and George bent to one knee. "This sword's name represents everything this department stands for, and it is my hope you continue to wield Iustitia in the pursuit of justice." Chief Adams tapped George on each shoulder with Iustitia. "Please rise, Acting

Officer Washington, and take your place among San Diego's finest."

A great cheer went up from the assembled crowd, and there were many handshakes and glad tidings. As the crowd dispersed, the chief spoke with George and Jeff privately.

"Well," the chief said, "I said I could help. Being an acting officer means you'll have no official duties, but you will be able to carry the side arm of your choice and have the full backing of the department should you need to arrest a criminal. If you wish to formalize this position, there are academy training programs available."

"My words fail me, Chief Adams," George said.

"Please, George, call me Bob," the chief said. "We are too far along in years to get hung up on titles. I have the feeling we are going to be spending time together periodically."

George smiled at Bob, bowed slightly, and stated, "Indeed!"

CHAPTER 18

One afternoon Jeff received a call from George. This was the very first call George had ever made to Jeff, so it was a landmark occasion. George was calling from the library, and he asked Jeff to meet him there. Jeff left quickly, and soon he was walking in the front door. He found George and Mrs. Witherspoon conversing at a table stacked with books.

As Jeff approached, Mrs. Witherspoon excused herself, and Jeff took her seat. "She still hates me, doesn't she?"

George replied, "Just a bit."

"What's up, George?"

"The more I study this nation's history, the more 'tis I understand the entire pursuit of the federal government has been to secure financial gain for a wealthy few," George said in amazement. "This country was founded so every citizen would have a chance to prosper and thrive. Thus far, especially in more recent decades, I see that government is no longer accountable to the people.

"During my speech of declination at the end of my last term, I spoke at length of the baneful effects of the Spirit of Party generally. I foresaw this Spirit, unfortunately, is inseparable from our nature, having it's root in the strongest of passions of the human mind. It exists in different shapes in all governments, more or less stifled, controlled, or repressed; but in those of the popular form it has seen the greatest rankness and is truly their worst enemy.

"The citizens have been lulled into such a profound state of apathy. Elected officials can convolute and pervert this government into anything that brings them the most financial gain. I find this state of affairs intolerable."

Jeff considered George's words carefully. "What are you going to do about it?"

"I feel as though I should march up to the steps of the Capitol and demand an explanation," George said vehemently.

"If you went there by yourself and started making demands, you would be arrested. If you insisted you were George Washington, you would be locked up in a mental institution," Jeff stated categorically. "However, if you gained the support of others, your chances of success would greatly increase."

"By what means could this be accomplished?" George asked.

"Acquiring support for people is what I do for a living. Just be aware that if your true origins come to light, I don't know what will happen."

"Uncertainty is part of life, is it not?" asked George.

"OK then, George. Let the new campaign of George Washington's march to the capital begin!" Jeff exclaimed. "The first thing is image," Jeff explained. "People need to recognize and identify with you and what you represent. Unlike the modern politician who only knows how to talk, though, your campaign is going to be based on action. From what I've seen, actions speak louder than words."

"Indeed they do, Jeffery," George confirmed.

"I want the politicians in Washington to focus their attention on me," Jeff continued. "I want them to believe this is an ordinary politically motivated gimmick to grab the public's attention. They should think you are simply an actor playing a part. We will reveal your true origins at the climax in the capital. If we do our jobs right, you will have sufficient popularity that the government won't dare make you disappear. You will have your opportunity to ask questions, George."

"As our campaign progresses," George said, "I should like to speak with the country's citizens to learn firsthand the issues they face. It shall be the ammunition I will use in my questioning in the capital."

Jeff asked, "What do you think about a little more formal attire for your everyday wear, George?"

"I have had thoughts in that direction, myself," George confessed. "'Twas what I was accustomed to in my days before my arrival. The garments I wore when we first met are considered common clothes in the past. Perhaps a more modern style of the same type of adornment would allow me to be more visually appealing. The application of a cocked hat would be most welcome. I seem to have lost mine during my travels."

"I suggest you go see Thom and work on getting your hair and face in shape," Jeff said. "If you give me the clothes you arrived in, I'll have an excellent tailor make you some updated versions."

"Very well then, Jeffery. I will meet you back at your dwelling later this evening."

"See you then, George."

Jeff departed then, and George went to find Mrs. Witherspoon to take his leave of her. After a few minutes searching the library, though, he found no trace of her. He asked one of the assistants where she might be, and the woman said she had taken some old periodicals to the recycling bins in the alley behind the library. The assistant pointed to the rear exit.

George exited the library and walked to the recycling bins. He found a pile of magazines strewn about, as if the person carrying them had suddenly dropped them.

A feeling of dread washed over George, and for the first time since his arrival, he feared someone he cared about was going to meet an untimely demise.

One end of the alley was blocked, so there was only one direction the culprits could have gone. Moving at a quickened pace, George made his way down the alley. Several other alleys joined the one behind the library at right angles, and it was difficult for George to choose which to pursue. Then he spotted a woman's shoe at the entrance of the second alley, so George moved swiftly down it.

Reaching the far end, George found another alley crossed in front of him. He looked in both directions and saw the first shoe's mate, so he sped in that direction.

As he traveled, he could hear the distant sound of a struggle and the periodic voice of a very angry woman. George pursued the sounds as fast as his feet could carry him, and when he rounded the next corner, he saw two young men struggling to put Mrs. Witherspoon in a car.

A quiet rage began to stir within George, and as he ran closer to the assailants, fury blinded him. As George leaped into the air, he withdrew Iustitia and brought his weapon of justice crashing down on the head of one of the men. The kidnapper dropped to the ground instantly after the blow.

Mrs. Witherspoon was between the other man and George. With his left hand, George grasped Mrs. Witherspoon by the arm, spun clockwise, and jerked her from the criminal's grip. Simultaneously, he swung Iustitia laterally to bring his weapon's full force to the side of the man's head. The recoil of the impact caused the would-be kidnapper's head to slam into the car's roof. This rendered him unconscious as well.

George and Mrs. Witherspoon had only a moment to take breaths, and then George heard the driver's door slam shut. The biggest black man George had ever seen walked around the front of the car to square off with him.

This man was a full head taller than George and outweighed him by at least one hundred pounds. His leather clothing and large amount of jewelry suggested this individual had great wealth.

George moved Mrs. Witherspoon to a position well behind him and stepped forward to confront the gargantuan. The huge man was sizing up George by trying to circle around him, but George stood his ground.

George was the first to speak. "You, sir, are rude and vile. If I may be so bold, the manner in which you dress dishonors the cattle it took to make such a garment!"

The man charged at George like some kind of demonic creature. When he drew near enough to George, Iustitia came to life and collided with the man's left cheek. The bone collapsed, but to George's astonishment, the criminal continued his charge. He drove straight through George and pushed him backward until he crashed into the alley wall. George lay there stunned, and Iustitia rested at his feet.

The mountain of a man picked the sword up and threw it across the alley into a Dumpster. With the strength of twenty men, he picked up George and hurled him into the Dumpster, as well. The man panted heavily from the exertion, shuffled to the front of the container, and peered inside. No doubt he wanted to finish off George. To his surprise, George seemed to have disappeared. The bewildered man began to look closely among the refuse. He pushed trash to the left and right to find any hint of George's presence.

With the speed of a missile, a small brass ball shot from the garbage and entered the massive man's right nostril. It lodged itself high in the man's sinus cavity. George rose from the trash like a phoenix, with his right hand on Iustitia's grip and the other a third of the way up the fiberglass rod, it arched like a fishing pole with a big, angry fish on the end of it. George put his left foot on the edge of the Dumpster to steady himself against the pull of his attacker.

The man grabbed the sword with both hands and tried to raise himself off Iustitia, but every time the rod straightened, it drove the ball farther into his nose. George kept so much tension on it that after a moment all the man could do was dangle there on his tippy-toes.

George held firm, and he grunted, "I suggest you yield, lest my sword pierce your brain—however small 'tis."

The enormous man said, "As soon as I get out of this, I'm gonna kill you and your bitch of a girlfriend!"

All at once a brick came sailing through the air and exploded on the back of the huge man's skull. The man staggered backward, which released Iustitia from his nose, and collapsed on his two accomplices. As George was trying to extricate himself from the dumpster, Clara walked over to where the big man had fallen. She saw him blinking and trying to regain his senses.

Without a moment's hesitation, she raised another brick above her head and brought it crashing down on his forehead. She bent at the waist and pointed at his bloody nose with a wrinkled index finger.

"Don't fuck with a librarian!" she shouted.

George was at her side a moment later. "Why, Mrs. Witherspoon, that was perfectly naughty!"

"Yes, it was, but I meant it in the most ladylike way," Clara said.

George was breathing heavily. "By the way, gentlemen," he stated firmly, "I would have you know I am arresting all of you. Furthermore, I am an officer of the law." George pointed to the badge on his shirt.

"You do know they are all unconscious, right?" Mrs. Witherspoon mentioned.

"Indeed," George affirmed. "However, since this is my first arrest, I wish to do things properly. Besides, I do not believe any of these men were inclined to hear what I had to say beforehand."

"You are correct, Mr. Washington. Perhaps a change of venue is in order," Mrs. Witherspoon said.

"I have one more duty to perform," said George. George flipped open his cell phone and hit the speed dial for Chief Adams. "Good day, Bob. I am sorry to disturb you, but it seems I have made my first arrest. I have need of you to tote these rather unsavory individuals to prison. I will let Mrs. Witherspoon provide the location."

CHAPTER 19

The paramedics had just finished checking George and Clara out when Jeff arrived. George had fared very well, considering his advanced years. A few bumps and bruises were all that remained. Mrs. Witherspoon suffered a couple broken nails and some severe annoyance.

"I can't leave you alone for a moment without having bodies piling up everywhere!" Jeff said.

"'Twas Mrs. Witherspoon's distress that caused me to act, Jeffery. Even with multiple assailants, we did win the day," George pointed out.

Mrs. Witherspoon simply stated, "The big one was mine."

Jeff shook his head with astonishment. Around that time, Chief Adams approached and said to the group, "Does anyone know who George and Mrs. Witherspoon clobbered today? His name is Terrance Rutherford George. He's a drug and prostitution kingpin known as King George. He's sometimes hired out to do some kidnapping on the side. For some reason, someone wanted Mrs. Witherspoon and hired these guys to snatch her."

George mused, "That name does sound a trifle familiar to me."

Jeff asked the chief, "Do you think this has anything to do with homeland security?"

"It's doubtful," the chief said. "It might be related to the three men George fought off rescuing that young woman—especially if they were gang members. It also means someone somewhere is watching you, so I would find the means to be elsewhere for a time."

"George and I are currently working on doing just that, but what about Mrs. Witherspoon?" Jeff asked.

George interjected, "I will take personal charge of Mrs. Witherspoon's safety—with your permission, madam." George bowed slightly to Clara.

"It seems as though I am to be forever ensnared by the ravages of associating with Mr. Thompson and Washington," Clara stated. "However, as Mr. Thompson's combat skills are as yet unknown, I will find refuge with Mr. Washington, provided proper accommodations are established."

"Very well, then," the chief concluded. "I will leave you under the protection of Acting Officer Washington and post additional people at your apartment building until you leave. Good luck, George. If you need anything else, just let me know."

George replied, "Thank you, Bob. Have a good evening."

The trio reentered the library, gathered Mrs. Witherspoon's personal effects, and then exited the front of the library. Franklin had been summoned for George and Mrs. Witherspoon, and Jeff took his car back to the apartment.

"Welcome back, G. Dub. Who's your fine lady friend?" Franklin said.

"Franklin, this is Mrs. Witherspoon. She is going to be my guest for a time," George said. "Mrs. Witherspoon, this is Franklin. He has been kind enough to convey me to various destinations in the past. Jeff has found him to have a special wisdom in dealing with the unsavory elements of society."

Mrs. Witherspoon looked at George. "Why did he address you as G. Dub?"

"'Tis a street name that has been granted me. 'Tis used as a term of endearment," explained George. "Do you have any knowledge of an individual named King George?" George asked Franklin.

"Sure, mon. He be a bad dude to be dealin' wit'. Crack, smack, and coke are how he be gettin' his money. Sometimes he takes womenfolk to work in his stable," Franklin said.

"Do you mean he owns horses, as well?" asked George.

"No, mon. I be sayin' he gets women for his brothel. Much unhappiness there, mon."

"Indeed", George replied "It would seem as though I *whacked* him earlier today when he tried to purloin Mrs. Witherspoon during a pitched battle."

"You killed him dead, mon? That be great news, G. Dub. Now things be lookin' up in the hood!" Franklin exclaimed.

"No, Franklin. You misunderstand," George said. "I did in fact arrest him and some of his minions."

"Oh. I be seein' now. You be meanin' 'busted' instead of 'whacked.' Sad times now, mon. He has big-money lawyers, so he won't be in jail long. Perhaps killin' is better in this case."

Franklin pulled up in front of the apartment building, and George said, "In our absence, would you continue to covertly monitor King George's lackeys? I daresay Mrs. Witherspoon's safety is paramount at this point."

"You can be countin' on me, mon."

George and Mrs. Witherspoon exited the cab and went to George's apartment. Upon entering the residence, George asked his guest to make herself comfortable in the living room.

George's apartment had a very Spartan look about it. There wasn't much refinement in the style of furnishings, and no artwork adorned the walls. The living areas were laid out similar to Jeff's place, but without a garage. His residence was still a work in progress, but George found it very comfortable.

After a few minutes, George entered the living room with a tray containing a pot of tea, a sugar bowl, and a container of cream. He set it down on the coffee table before Mrs. Witherspoon.

"After our unfortunate experience this afternoon, I hope a hot cup of tea will dispel any lingering trepidations."

"I do thank you, Mr. Washington, for your hospitality and protection. This sort of valor is uncommon in my experience," Mrs. Witherspoon said.

"Please call me George, if you will. We are going to be spending some time together, so perhaps a little less formality will make the time pass more smoothly."

"Your point is valid, George. Please call me Clara. After dinner," Clara continued, "we should speak about some ground rules for my stay in your company."

"Very well, Clara. Do you have a preference for dinner?" George asked.

"Something light would do well," Clara replied.

"Do soup and a salad sound appetizing?" George asked.

"It shall do nicely," agreed Clara.

"Then I will prepare a sumptuous repast, but first I should make some effort to cleanse myself. My clothes and person have the air of having traveled. I shall return shortly. Please enjoy your tea."

Then George departed. After about forty-five minutes, George reappeared and declared dinner was served. They both sat at the dining table and ate their meals quietly.

A cloud of uncertainty filled the room. After George finished and cleared the dishes, he broke it by saying, "My guest room has been prepared for you, and on the morrow I will summon Franklin to help us retrieve the necessities from your home. I have placed some of my loungewear for you to slumber in on the bed in your room. You will no doubt be quite becoming while wearing them."

"This is the first time I've stayed in another residence since Mr. Witherspoon's passing," Clara admitted. "To be clear, I will not tolerate impropriety of any kind. Am I understood, George?"

"If it would make you feel more secure, I will place two bricks at your bedside for your use, should the need arise," George said.

For the first time since George had met Clara, she actually managed a rudimentary smile. "That shan't be necessary, George, but thank you."

"Then I will take my leave of you," George said wearily. "Feel free to explore the apartment. Should you have a need, just knock on my door. Good night, Clara."

Clara said good night, and George left for his bedroom.

CHAPTER 20

Chief Adams walked into the security room at the county hospital and stood at the foot of the bed in which King George had been restrained. The villain had two black eyes, and his nose was swollen like a cucumber. He had also suffered traumas to the back and front of his head.

"The King" was conscious, but his massive headache put him in a surly mood. Chief Adams opened the dialogue.

"You let an old man stick a bicycle flagpole up your nose and an elderly librarian club you with a brick. Twice. You are a pitiful excuse of a criminal, Terrance, and now you're laid up here with a laundry list of charges to answer for. Would you mind telling me who hired you to snatch that old lady, or would you like me to let a Girl Scout come in here and rough you up some more?"

"My lawyers are going to have me out of here in a matter of hours, Adams. I don't have to tell you nothing! By the way, my name is King George, so get it right," Terrance responded.

"What exactly are you the king of, Terrance? The king of pain? Flagpole snorting? Maybe you're the king of brick facials. That old librarian did you a favor and improved your looks considerably."

"You won't be such a smartass once I get out of here, Adams," Terrance growled.

"Threatening me is only digging a deeper hole for you to climb out of," Adams replied. "You can fess up and strike a deal with the prosecutor, or I can send you and your two girlfriends down the deepest hole I can find for the rest of your lives. It's your choice, Terrance."

The prisoner did not respond, so Chief Adams left the room. He made certain there were sufficient officers stationed outside the room, and he spoke to the doctor to ensure Terrance wouldn't be leaving for a long time due to medical concerns.

Something about this case didn't smell right to the chief. Terrance made tons of money with all the rackets he was involved with. Why would he take the chance of losing it all by snatching an old lady?

There had to be a huge payoff to warrant such a risk, or maybe someone had dirt on him. Perhaps he had no alternative. Usually if anyone tried to best Terrance, that person ended up taking a dirt nap in a very remote location.

There were still pieces missing to this puzzle. It seemed as though the chief needed to poke his nose deeper into

Terrance's business. Then an idea came to the chief, and he immediately headed for the psych ward. He arrived outside a familiar door and knocked quietly until he heard a soft voice say, "Come in."

The chief took a seat at the side of the bed and said, "How are you feeling today, Agent Hancock?"

"Better than when all this started. The nightmares aren't as bad as they used to be. Thank you for stopping in from time to time, Chief Adams," Phil responded.

"I know George only spoke with you once, but I believe he thinks well of you," the chief said.

"He gave me a lot to think about, and his visit did make it easier to deal with my issues," Phil admitted.

The chief asked, "Has anyone from the Department of Homeland Security contacted you at all?"

"The director called a week or two after this started. He said when the doctor released me, I was to report to his office for a debriefing," Phil stated.

"That sounds kind of cold. Don't they have a special medical facility set aside for agents?" asked the chief.

"They probably think one psych ward is the same as another," Phil said sadly.

"Did any family members contact you?" the chief asked.

"I have no family to speak of, just one sibling who thinks I'm a freak. Other than that, it's just been me and my computers. Now I don't even have that," Phil said mournfully.

"That's precisely the reason I'm here today," the chief continued. "George has gotten himself into a bit of trouble, and I could really use your help to get him out of it. Are you interested?"

Phil's mood seemed to lighten a bit. "Of course, Chief. What do you need?"

"If you would be willing, I'll see if I can get the doctor to release you for a few hours each day to my custody," Chief Adams said. "I'll take you to the department mainframe, where you can help me find some answers. This is on the QT, Phil. Both of us could be in hot water if we go too far. Wouldn't you agree?"

"Yes, Chief. I found that out the hard way," Phil recalled.

"OK then. I'll make the arrangements. Is Agent McFearson still here?" the chief queried.

"The doctor said he was released a couple weeks ago," Phil informed the chief. "Since no charges could be filed against him because of his agent status, he simply left."

"I guess we'll have to deal with that later. Get ready, Phil. I'll be back in a while," Chief Adams concluded.

CHAPTER 21

Several days had passed since King George was apprehended. Clara had retrieved vital possessions from her home and was becoming a welcomed presence in George's ever-increasing social group.

Even though Jeff had a considerable amount of wealth, they would need much more if George was going to make it all the way to the capital. Jeff spent days talking on the phone, going to meetings, and trying to convince those he had helped become rich and powerful to back his cause.

George spent his time watching out for Clara and listening to bits of information that filtered his way through Franklin. One morning as George and Clara were finishing breakfast, they heard a knock on the door. When George answered, he saw Jeff.

"Good morning, Jeff. How may I help you this morning?"

"Well, George, a both timely and unique opportunity has presented itself," Jeff said. "It appears as though the press has gotten wind of your apprehension of King George, and a large mob of reporters has gathered outside the lobby. They are waiting for you to tell the story. We've had no time to prepare for questions, and we don't know what the official police report says, but this could be the perfect launching point for your campaign. Do you think you can pull off a press conference at this time?"

"I have had dealings with crowds before," George stated boldly. "How do you wish to proceed?"

"Put on one of the sets of clothes I had made for you. Be sure you have Iustitia at your side. Then simply tell the story as it happened, and we'll see where it takes us."

"Very well, Jeffery. I will be with you shortly," George stated firmly.

George retreated to his bedroom, where he donned a pair of light-gray knee-length cotton pants, white stockings, and black leather riding boots that reached to the top of his calf. His shirt was white cotton with just a hint of ruffles at the cuffs and from the middle of the chest up to the starched collar. Over the shirt he wore a light-brown vest with brass buttons and a gold watch fob. As always, Iustitia was securely fastened at his left side.

When George turned to leave his room, Clara was standing in the doorway. George said, "Engaging in a bit of impropriety, Clara?"

"Not at all, George," Clara exclaimed. "Shame on you for thinking such a thing! I have no wish to see you go out in front of God and man looking a fright!"

With that she stepped forward, straightened his collar, and made sure his mock ruffles were running in a straight line on the front of his shirt.

"I know very little of your and Mr. Thompson's business, but I do know kindness when I see it. I daresay you and your associate are kind to a fault. Please be careful in all you do," Clara said. George smiled, and Clara said, "Don't forget this."

She pinned his officer's badge to the left side of his vest. George took her hand, kissed it, set his cocked hat upon his head, and softly said, "I shall return."

Then he left to join Jeff. News vans were parked along the entire length of the street outside the building. Someone had set up a small podium. It had microphones from every news agency in the city. Newspaper and magazine reporters were all clambering over each other to get a story.

George and Jeff paused in the lobby for a moment. George looked at Jeff, who seemed rather dubious. He put his hand on Jeff's shoulder and said, *"Audentes fortuna iuvat."* Jeff looked at George with a puzzled expression, and George translated. "Fortune favors the bold."

"In modern times, we say, 'Let's rock,'" Jeff replied.

Jeff assisted George in pushing his way to the podium. Once there, Jeff stepped to the microphones. He stood there quietly looking out over the crowd, and for three or four minutes, the din continued. Then the ruckus ceased, and Jeff spoke.

"Ladies and gentlemen, my name is Jeffery Thompson. I am a professional lobbyist. Three years ago, the Department of Homeland Security investigated me. During that time, I had every aspect of my life exposed for all to see. At the conclusion of the case, it was determined I had broken no laws and committed no crime. Yet I was subjected to the rigors of an investigation as if I had.

"Three years later," Jeff continued, "I found the same thing happening again as part of another investigation. The details are still a mystery and classified. Now this overzealous and aggressive style of investigation has come to affect my business partner and friend. He is a man who has a great deal to say, and I believe this country's citizens need to hear it. I have found him to have a special wisdom and insight into the political and social affairs of this nation. You no doubt have heard various rumors and stories concerning his apprehension of Terrance George, but there is much more to the story than just a simple altercation, so perhaps it's time for him to set the record straight. Ladies and gentlemen, I give you George Washington."

A round of applause went up, and George took the stand. In his riding boots and hat, he towered over the people in attendance.

When the applause died down, George removed his hat as a sign of respect for the assemblage of people. Then he began to speak.

"'Tis true. My name is, in fact, George Washington. I know many of you find it curious my name is the same as the man from this country's historical accounts. That is a matter for another time.

"'Tis also true what Master Jeffery has said. There is a great deal more to tell than one might believe. There is darkness prevalent throughout this nation. I wish not to be an alarmist, but I believe it extends into the governing body, as well.

"The citizens of this land have always had the power to effect change and root out those individuals who seek to gain at the expense of freedom and personal liberty, but the citizens also lack the conviction and desire necessary to maintain this government the way it was meant to be.

"Perhaps those who reside in this land feel they can offer nothing of value to perpetuate the cause of freedom and justice, but to them I say nay! An average citizen can and must pursue the rights of the just daily. Otherwise, they are simply cattle to be led about from pasture to pasture.

"Today's social convention considers me a senior citizen. I am meant to be past my prime and of little value to my community. However, when foul-minded youths sought to accost a young maiden, I found the means to come to her aid and show that criminal behavior is unwelcome here.

"More recently, yet another criminal element sought to abduct a very dear friend, Mrs. Clara Witherspoon, the presiding librarian here in San Diego. As difficult as 'tis to believe, 'twas she who struck the final blow in a pitched battle that convinced King George to yield. She is a vision of loveliness, and though her years are as many as mine, she let these lesser men know in no uncertain terms their behavior was rude and not to be tolerated.

"Those homeland security agents who sought to apprehend me unjustly in an ill-conceived and reckless manner found that personal pride and authority-related impunity does not bode well for them in some circumstances.

"I do not condemn the officials at the Department of Homeland Security or their agents. I do not bear them malice of any kind. Their task is a great one, and I support their efforts fully. However, in some instances their agents go too far and tread upon the liberties and rights the Constitution grants us all. 'Tis my desire to work more closely with them to help ensure these instances are few."

The assembled crowed was stunned. George's speech, although in an older vernacular, was getting through. His every word transfixed everyone in attendance.

"The local constabulary did notice my efforts to ensure my safety, as well as that of my friends. Police Chief Adams thought well enough to bestow the position of acting officer upon me —a title and responsibility I consider sacred.

"These examples I provided are of what people can accomplish when they put their willingness and desire to live free into action. Mrs. Witherspoon and I are advanced in years, but even so, we did make a difference.

"At a near future time, 'tis my desire to travel to the capital and inquire of this nations government why so many unfavorable conditions exist. Why has this governing institution strayed so far from the original designers' plan?

"I would ask that if you believe as I believe, and if you desire the same accountability as I desire, join me in my journey of discovery. Together we will find the answers we seek. Be certain of this, those who would come, 'tis not an armed conflict I seek.

"We are all Americans, and such actions would be counterproductive to our cause. All I require is your presence and knowledge to arm me for my eventual dialogue with those in the capital. When we arrive in sufficient numbers, our voices will be heard, and the true nature of the government of the United States of America will be revealed.

"My friend Mr. Thompson will have more information as the quest continues. Now I will answer a few questions. Please be brief and courteous."

A forest of hands shot into the air, and George pointed at a young female reporter in the front row. "What is your question, miss?"

"Mr. Washington, I'm Sandra Knocks from KQRH Radio. It sounds as though you are calling for people to form groups of vigilantes. Is that what you're advocating?"

"Ms. Knocks, let us explore that statement for a moment. In this nation's earliest days, no police force existed to deal with criminals and outlaws. Those responsibilities fell to the men of the community. They had to keep a watchful eye on strangers and goings-on to discern whether they created a threat for the public. The men charged with this responsibility had to be vigilant at it—hence the name 'vigilante.'

"Just like the Department of Homeland Security and other law enforcement organizations, some individuals have an unfortunate tendency to go too far. Whether 'tis the intoxication of the authority they are granted or some personal gain they desire, those who abuse their offices place a stigma on the entire institution. That is why the term 'vigilante' is reviled and spoken with disdain.

"During my time here, I have worked well with Chief Adams and the director of the Department of Homeland Security, and I shall continue to do so. Freedom, security, and peace of mind start at home, Ms. Knocks."

George pointed to a television reporter in the second row.

"Mr. Washington, I'm Alan Hamilton from KNITV San Diego. King George is a well-known killer and mobster. Aren't you worried about reprisals from his accomplices?"

George answered, "I wish to make it known there is nothing kingly about Terrance Rutherford George. He is a thief and a liar, and his absence will bring a more pleasant mood to the public. To the point of his lieutenants, I can only say this—should they desire to be members in good standing of this city and be kind and courteous to all, then they should fear me not. Should they wish to bring harm to me or those I care about, I shall use whatever means necessary to seek them out and subject them to the wrath of Mrs. Witherspoon."

There was a great amount of laughter throughout the crowd. George picked another reporter.

"Mr. Washington, I'm Jimmy Madison of the *City News*. The style of your clothing looks very old as is the way you speak. Why do you want to appear so antiquated?"

"Mr. Madison, I dress and speak as I always have. I do wear more modern attire occasionally, but I am quite comfortable in this raiment. I see you have no trouble understanding my manner of speaking, so I see no reason to alter it."

George indicated another.

"Mr. Washington, I'm a journalist from a magazine called *Weapons Weekly*. I noticed you carry a sword at your side. I don't recognize the make of it. What is its origin?"

"Sir, this side arm carries with it the name Iustitia. 'Tis a weapon of my own design and build. It has served me valiantly through a number of battles. Its origin is meager—a child's flagpole, a kitchen implement, and a piece from a broken chair. You will find, my good fellow, that nearly anything can be used as a weapon. What matters most is how it is used and the integrity of the one wielding it."

George went on for nearly half an hour fielding questions and relating stories of his recent conflicts. Like a master orator, he carefully maneuvered around those inquiries into his background.

George concluded. "I mean to reinstate what the founders of this great nation fought for, sacrificed for, and paid dearly for. I ask all people within the sound of my voice to stand with me on that day and renew the spirit that made this country great. Thank you, one and all."

CHAPTER 22

Chief Adams's phone rang, and it was the doctor who had been working on Terrance's wounds. He reported that late the night before, the officers who had been guarding Terrance had been rendered unconscious, and his patient had escaped. The escape wasn't noticed until morning rounds were conducted. A search of the entire facility by hospital security found only the unconscious police officers. After speaking with the doctor, Chief Adams went back to see whether Phil had made any progress.

"So, Phil, we've been at this a week. What have you uncovered so far?" asked Chief Adams.

"Terrance George has spent his adult life in and out of prison," Phil reported. "He used to be one of four trusted aides recruited out of prison for the William Howe crime family, but the other three and Howe himself were killed by some accidental beheadings. Terrance's statement to the police was, 'It must have been a virus.' There wasn't enough evidence to arrest him.

"The FBI became involved when it was discovered he was importing narcotics and weapons and engaging in human trafficking." Phil paused. "You might find this of interest, Chief. Only one law enforcement agent has gone up against Terrance and survived. Care to guess who?"

"I don't have a clue, Phil," the chief stated.

"Agent Dan McFearson. Apparently, he did a few years with the FBI before he joined the Department of Homeland Security." Phil went on. "In his altercation with Terrance, he was nearly killed. Dan was out of commission for six months while recuperating from his wounds. Shortly thereafter, he changed jobs."

"Knowing Dan the way you do, do you think he'd like another crack at taking Terrance down?" the chief asked.

While Phil was supposed to be in the hospital, he had to be discreet when inquiring about Agent McFearson. However, he did find out that Agent Marlin, Dan, and he had been put on administrative leave after the conflict with George, so it would be a bit tougher to track Dan down.

"Dan does like to brag and bluster about his fighting skills and collars he's made, so I believe he would help us. I do find it curious he's never mentioned his near-death experience to me before," Phil said.

"See if you can locate Agent McFearson. If he is as tenacious as you say, he could be an asset," the chief advised.

Chief Adams went back to his office. There were a few other cases that required his attention, but even as he worked, something still bothered him. A few hours later, Chief Adams returned to Phil and said, "It's almost time for me to take you back to the hospital, Phil. We'll try some more tomorrow. Thank you for everything."

On the trip to the hospital, the chief said, "From what the doctor says, you're making great progress in your recovery. Have you had any thoughts about what you might do after you're discharged?"

"I'm not looking forward to resuming the spy business," Phil confessed. "I told Agent Marlin I'd never been part of an apprehension before, and he still sent me to that apartment. I even had to borrow a gun from Agent McFearson. How pitiful is that? Just so you understand, Chief, there are a lot more agents like Marlin out there. They couldn't care less about anyone as long as they get to assert themselves."

"As you're considering your future plans," Chief Adams said, "just know I can make a place for you here if you wish. It's not as prestigious as homeland security, and Lord knows the money isn't nearly as good, but what I can guarantee you is that information acquisition will be your only task. You'll have friends you can count on and digital action in abundance."

"That does sound pretty good," Phil conceded. "I will certainly consider it. Thanks, Chief."

The chief escorted Phil back to his room and consulted briefly with the doctor. With his current progress, Phil would most likely be discharged in two weeks. Chief Adams thanked the doctor and headed back to the station.

The chief pulled into the police parking deck and found his reserved space. He exited the car and walked to the elevator. After he pressed the up button, the doors opened, and he stepped inside. The elevator already held one occupant when the doors opened.

It was a police sergeant who was rather small in stature. His uniform didn't seem to fit him very well. Portions of it seemed somewhat baggy in areas. Other than that, the sergeant was within regulations, and Chief Adams didn't give it a second thought until the man said, "What floor will you be wantin', Chief?"

The chief spun around and tried to bring his gun up on the man, but he found a pistol already pointed at his face.

"I'd be puttin' that gun back where it belongs there, Chiefy."

Then the man pressed the stop button on the elevator. Chief Adams returned his gun to its holster. "You must be Agent McFearson."

Dan put his gun away. "I'm only here to talk, Chief, so don't be gettin' any notions, me fine fellow."

"Perhaps you would care to join me in my office. I think that would be the best place to talk, don't you?" the chief asked.

"Aye, Chief. You got a point there."

Dan released the elevator, and the two men continued to the chief's office on the sixth floor. Once in the office, both men found their respective seats.

"You know somethin', Chief? I been here walkin' about for over an hour, and not one person asked who I was."

"I'll have to look into that, Agent. What's on your mind?" asked the chief.

"I know ye been spendin' time with Phil. I know you have him workin' on a case of some kind. What I wanna know is why."

"Because of George," the chief stated. "I've come to know George Washington over a period of time. He has earned my respect and admiration, and he is a far kinder man than one would expect in this day and age. George seemed to believe in Phil's capacity to overcome the trauma of the incident at Mr. Thompson's apartment, and he gave

Phil the confidence to succeed. As a result, Phil's due to be discharged soon.

"I'm certain George was hoping," Chief Adams continued, "you would pursue a kinder, gentler course and not go down the road of vengeance like Agent Marlin. So…what's it going to be, Agent? Are you going to choose Agent Marlin's course of action or do something a bit nobler and help Phil and I keep a drug lord from killing George and his friends?"

"Let me tell you somethin' about your friend Mr. Washington," Dan said. "When I first got to Mr. Thompson's apartment, I managed to lift some of George's fingerprints and DNA from a glass in the kitchen. Sure enough, that was when Phil got hurt and I got me arse handed to me. When I was released, me fellows in Washington ran the prints and DNA and couldn't find no match at all. Interpol, CIA, NSA, IRS, and MI6 all had no records. That be sayin' to me this man be an agent of a kind that don't want to be recognized," Dan concluded.

"Then why did he hold a press conference three days ago announcing his plans to lead a group of citizens to Washington to speak to the White House?" the chief asked. "That doesn't seem very low profile to me."

"I didn't know that, Chief. I ain't gotta clue who this man is at all now."

"I want you to consider something long and hard over the next few days, Agent McFearson," the chief said. "In the time George has been here, he has survived three attacks on his person, put himself at risk defending others, and helped an ailing agent find some peace after a traumatic experience. Does it really matter who he is? He could be the real George Washington raised from the dead for all I know," the chief continued. "Also, he arrested a drug lord—someone you have had dealings with before by the name of Terrance Rutherford George."

"Now you be pullin' me leg, Chief," Dan exclaimed. "That big son of a bitch likened to kill me years ago."

"Well, with a little help from an elderly female librarian, George not only knocked Terrance's ass out but two of his cronies, as well. How does that make you feel, Agent?" the chief asked sternly.

"It be pissin' me right the hell off, Chief!" Dan growled.

"Let that burn in really good, Agent McFearson," Chief Adams said. "There are three outcomes I can see. One, you're in a position to help a kind old man get rid of a longtime scumbag. Two, you can go after George like Agent Marlin and kill him, but remember there's no fortune or glory in killing an old man. Three, George beats you again, and you suffer the shame of having a senior citizen best you twice. What's more desirable?"

"If you already have him, what do ya need me for?" questioned Dan.

The Chief put both hands on his desk, stood, and leaned across the desk. He glared at Agent McFearson and said intently, "Someone broke him out of the security wing of the hospital last night."

Dan's face began to turn red with rage as the news hit home.

Chief Adams concluded the meeting. "What I do know and can say with absolute certainty is that George is my friend, and he deserves all the privileges of being my friend." Chief Adams smiled and sat back down. "It is, of course, your choice, Agent. However, should any harm befall George and I find out you're responsible, there will be a reckoning."

"I take your meanin', Chief. Don't ya be worryin' about that. No matter what you might know about me, I be only interested in the bad guys."

"Then I believe we're finished here," Chief Adams announced. "Please call before you drop in again, Agent McFearson."

CHAPTER 23

After a few weeks of effort, Jeff managed to raise the necessary campaign funds. As he would for a political fund raiser, he invited the members of Congress on his client list and all the well-known business tycoons he could find to a social event at a country club. George was wearing his retro-style military dress uniform while he moved about the floor meeting and greeting the individuals Jeff introduced him to.

The country club hosting the gathering was an opulent structure. Its grounds were vast, and they offered many verandas and outdoor amenities.

One of the senators commented to Jeff, "Your associate George is a remarkable fellow! During his opening speech and the later conversations I've been involved with, he hasn't fallen out of character once. It's almost like having the real George Washington right here."

"George knows everything about the first president of this country so well that it is infused in the very way he thinks. If anyone can raise awareness of political issues, he certainly can," Jeff replied.

One of the representatives from California that Jeff knew very well had pulled George aside for a private conversation.

"Mr. Washington, I must say you look absolutely stunning in your uniform. Your taste in retro styles is simply fabulous!"

"Thank you, sir, for your kind words," George said politely. "'Tis a garment my friend Jeffery had designed by a craftsman named Armani. Comfort seems to have been sewn in every stitch."

"You know, George, there are many amenities at this club that are conducive to comfort, as well. There are lovely walking paths and terraces one could do some serious swinging on," the man stated.

"Indeed," George said. "I used to swing at my estate in Virginia quite often—mostly on the front porch. Sometimes I did so with business associates while closing agreements. Other times the servants would bring me a brandy or two, and I would allow them to swing with me for a while."

"My goodness, George," the man said. "You're a regular party animal. I would consider it no small favor if you and I did a little swinging ourselves."

"Excuse me, Congressman. I shall return in a moment," George replied nervously. George walked over to Jeff. "Jeffery, the congressman you introduced me to is, I believe, regarding me in an odd way. How should I respond?"

"What did he say?" Jeff inquired.

"Something about going for a walk and swinging out on a terrace. Is this another instance of someone being overly happy, as we have discussed before?"

"George, the congressman is gay—just like Thom. You still look confused," Jeff observed.

"Indeed," George replied. "When I make mention that a person seems gay, I refer to one's disposition and joyous demeanor. To what do you refer?" George asked.

Jeff looked around to see if anyone was within earshot. Then he leaned toward George's ear and told him in the most basic terms what it meant to be gay in modern society. George had an astonished expression.

His temper began to flare, and he said, "This man believes me to be a sodomite! I shall give him an earful that will cause his ancestors to grimace with discomfort!"

Jeff grabbed George by the arm and pulled him closer. "Hang on a moment, George. You've been understanding with everyone you've encountered thus far, but now you're angered because a gay congressman believes you handsome enough to want to spend quality time with you. This man has been a congressman longer than I've been alive. He can help us with our campaign, but not if you storm over there and cause a scene."

"I do not believe my gentlemanly virtues will serve me well on this occasion," George admitted.

"On the contrary," Jeff insisted. "Treat him as you would a young maiden who might have suggested a similar activity, but be sure to spin it positively in the end and ask for his support. Gay people are nothing more than another type of class or culture that makes up this country. We will talk in greater detail about this after our guests have gone."

"It would seem that I do not have as good a grasp on modern affaires as I presumed. I am feeling a measure of discomfort concerning this revelation, but I will accept your wisdom on the matter. Jeffery, you are truly wise beyond your years," George conceded.

After returning to the representative, George stated politely, "Congressman, the swinging you propose would no doubt be a grand time indeed. However, even though I am not currently betrothed, I am attempting to gain favor with a woman of immense beauty and distinction. I do wish you well with your swinging efforts. I hope what you have heard here this evening has convinced you to support my efforts to bring a positive change to the nation and its citizens. We have much to gain by the attempt."

"George, my friend," the man announced, "it's a rare event when someone turns me down, but I must say I respect you and the gracious manner with which you declined my offer. If you have a need, just have Mr. Thompson contact my aide. If it is within my power, I will help you all I can."

George bowed slightly to the congressman and gratefully said, "Thank you for your support, congressman. Please excuse me."

Because of Jeff's contacts and George's diplomacy, Jeff was able to secure the financial backing for the campaign. He leased a motor home for the trip, secured venues in a number of cities along the way, and bought airtime for public service announcements. The local mayors were delighted to have all the free attention drawn to their cities, and they made Jeff and George's entourage feel very welcome. Jeff hoped that as George's popularity increased, some prominent celebrities and news organizations would ask to interview him.

The exposure of the initial press conference generated a great deal of excitement among San Diego's citizens. George's exploits fending off criminals and homeland security had earned George a small cult following. The fanfare reached its peak while the RV was exiting the city. George saw a crowd of several hundred people on both sides of the highway ramp. They were cheering and holding up signs that read, "Go get 'em, G. Dub," "G. Dub Rocks," and "G. Dub for President Again!" Franklin and the young woman George had helped had obviously influenced people.

Jeff, George, and Clara were finally out on their adventure. There were two support vehicles in the form of small box trucks that carried sound equipment, wardrobe items, and some creature comforts for Clara trailing behind the RV. People who had been hired as private security for George and Clara drove the trucks and RV. With Terrance and Agent Marlin lurking about, it seemed prudent.

George was as good as his word and rarely left Clara's side. The two seemed to be enjoying the pleasure of each other's company thoroughly. On those instances when George had to speak publicly, Clara fussed after him to be certain he was looking his best in the public eye. She would still give Jeff a hard time periodically, but it was mostly in jest.

The first stop was Phoenix, Arizona. The amphitheater Jeff had leased was fairly small. It only held about two thousand people. After their arrival, it was only a matter of hours before the stage was set and the guests started to arrive. Jeff was a nervous wreck, and he fretted over the smallest details.

George was calmly passing the time with Clara when Jeff approached him. "This is your big night, George. Shouldn't you be rehearsing your speech?"

"I know what 'tis I wish to say, Jeffery. The premise and message I bring hasn't changed since the beginning. Would constant rehearsal enhance it to any degree?" George asked.

"It might," Jeff said impatiently.

"Calm yourself, Jeffery," George insisted. "You will not survive this journey if you fall into a dither upon our first engagement."

Jeff began a series of deep, cleansing breaths, and after a few moments, he seemed to regain his composure. He thanked George for his advice and left to finish his tasks.

Soon all was ready for George to address the crowd. The houselights were lowered, and Jeff took the stage. He began the evening.

"Ladies and gentlemen, every person assembled here has one thing in common. We're all Americans! For many years I have been helping various political agencies convince everyone to vote one way or another, and in all that time, I've seen that the elected officials in the capital have diminishing regard for the average citizen. They are more interested in asserting themselves here and abroad.

"I felt powerless to do anything about it until I met one man who changed my way of thinking. He showed me that those who started this country were great and wise, and this government will work the way it's supposed to if those who we put in governing offices will let it. Please welcome George Washington!"

Thunderous applause went up, and George strode onto the stage. He was dressed in a blue and white military uniform of vintage design with all the detail of his original uniform from two centuries before. Featured prominently on the left breast of his uniform jacket was the officer's shield Chief Adams had awarded him. It was polished to a high sheen. On the left side of his waist, as always, was Iustitia in an equally shiny state. Jeff had outfitted George with a wireless microphone carefully concealed beneath his jacket collar.

George stood at center stage with no lectern before him. There were no microphone stands or even a chair to sit on. He had said beforehand he didn't want any distractions from his message.

"Citizens of the United States of America," George started, "please harken unto my words. Bring your attention and national pride to bear upon what I am about to say!" George paused for a moment before continuing. "I am George Washington, he who helped to found this nation eleven score and eighteen years ago, he who fought in countless engagements to rid the land of British oppressors, and he who served as military general and first president!"

George removed his military dress hat and held it under his left arm at his waist. He turned slowly and began to walk across the front of the stage.

"There are many souls in attendance this evening. It might be that you believe I have no knowledge of modern times and the issues the citizens of this land face. I can assure all who hear me I am uniquely aware of your sorrows and their causes.

"No grand miracle spawned the formation of this country overnight. No deity brought this country forth with a mere word. There was, however, much pain, suffering, and loss of life in the pursuit of liberty. I have borne witness to all of that, and now that we have had our full measure for many years, I find that lesser elements of the nation we built are corrupting the principles the founders set forth.

"In my era, those communities of sufficient size to warrant sending representatives to the capital would send trusted individuals to speak on their behalf, individuals with vested personal interests but who were also mindful of the welfare of the areas from whence they came.

"Currently, congressional representatives might have residence in the districts they represent, but they are so far afield from the friends and neighbors they speak for that they could not possibly know their constituents' needs. Unless the representatives make themselves available to speak to their neighbors directly, there can be no proper communication."

George paused, and a loud round of applause swept over the crowd. After the din diminished, George continued. "My previous statement also presupposes that the people for whom the government was made are willing to participate in upholding the created laws and voting with their best consciences at the polls. A serious absence of voters exists today. Are the Americans of this land so caught up in the technology of the times and the pursuit of instant gratification that the affairs of state should be ignored? I say nay!

"Daily should the zeal be wrought forth in keeping all branches of government working as is proper, ensuring that the needs of the people are met with the same frequency as putting one's shoes on in the morning. These actions should be paramount."

Jeff and Clara stood offstage and watched George as he walked back and forth across the front of the stage with his hat under one arm. He gestured emphatically with the other. Not once did George ever take his eyes off the audience. On many occasions it seemed as though he locked vision with individuals as he stressed a number of points.

George came to the part of his speech concerning the security officials and overzealous agents. "In January of 1756, I addressed the officers of the Virginia Regiment. I told them to remember that it is the actions, and not the commission, that make the officer. I told them there was more expected from them than the title.

"My recent experiences with homeland security and other law enforcement agencies have proven there can be no justice if officers of the law assert themselves for the intoxicating thrill of dominion over another. There is no reason I am aware of to prevent citizens from working in concert with this nation's security agents to ensure peace and the American way of life will always remain."

George spoke for an hour on a wide range of subjects. The overall atmosphere of the group was positive. When George had critical things to say about the government, there were thunderous cheers, and when he had criticisms about the country's people, the celebratory mood diminished. However, George made his points so well there were no means by which to argue.

George concluded his speech. "Some time ago, about 1757, I wrote a letter to the speaker of the Virginia House of Burgesses, and it is the thought I will leave with you this evening. 'I have diligently sought the public welfare; and have endeavored to inculcate the same principles on all that are under me. These reflections will be a cordial to my mind so long as I am able to distinguish between good and evil.' Thank you, ladies and gentlemen, for your gracious attention."

A standing ovation was instantly at hand. George performed one of his very gentlemanly bows, placed his hat upon his head, and walked confidently from the stage. He looked ten feet tall.

Jeff and Clara met up with George and congratulated him for a wonderful speech. Jeff shook his hand, and Clara stood up on her toes and kissed him on the cheek.

CHAPTER 24

"This is John Rutledge for K1701 news. George Washington's pseudo political speech rocked the amphitheater here in Phoenix last night. Washington is a tribute speaker who first captured the attention of San Diego's citizens by battling the criminal forces of that region.

"There were also rumors the Department of Homeland Security attempted to arrest this George Washington look-alike but were foiled in the attempt. Officials at the agency headquarters in Washington refuse to comment.

"Listeners phoning the station had comments ranging from adulation to irritation. G. Dub, as his fans in San Diego call him, had both scathing and high praise for this nation's government and the people who reside here. A number of patrons were asked to sit down and speak with G. Dub and his manager, Jeffery Thompson, after the speech to get their views of the government's current state.

"G. Dub and his manager hope that as their cross-country trip continues, those citizens who feel the same as this group of travelers will join them in Washington to speak to the president. The White House has not yet commented on the news.

"The overall message everyone gathered was that this country has deviated from its founders' plan, and for it to survive, some changes have to be made. This is John Rutledge for K1701 news. Back to the studios."

President Saunders sat in the conference room at the Department of Homeland Security headquarters and listened as this broadcast concluded. Director Pierce Butler waited in anticipation for the president's comments.

"What you're telling me, Director Butler, is the same old man who beats the hell out of criminals and your agents with a stick is now on his way to Washington to talk to me?"

"It would seem so, Mr. President," the director stated.

"Who is this guy? Where did he come from? If someone is gathering a force of people in order to coerce me into speaking with him, then perhaps a few details are in order, don't you think, Director Butler?" asked the president.

"I agree, Mr. President. As it turns out, Agent McFearson managed to get some prints and DNA from Mr. Thompson's apartment before he was incapacitated. We ran the prints and DNA through all known databases. There were no results at all. Facial recognition software and voiceprint analysis all came back negative." Butler continued. "Every spy and criminal I have ever dealt with has based their illegal activities on staying out of the spotlight and under the radar. Mr. Washington, whatever his agenda, has sought out media and public attention."

The president sat there with his hand on his shaking forehead.

"Washington's apprehension of the known drug lord Terrance George might have made him a hero, but he's also put his own life in serious jeopardy—especially since George escaped custody at the hospital in San Diego. If there is even a small amount of truth to Terrance's reputation, Washington might not make it here at all," Butler concluded.

Saunders sat quietly for a few moments before speaking. "What do we know for certain about Washington and his group?"

"We have started a psych profile on Washington, and I've brought the files for Thompson and Mrs. Witherspoon that we had compiled from our first encounter with them." The director started his report. "Jeffery Thompson is a very successful lobbyist who has a master's in political science and a master's in psychology. Even though some politicians he has helped pass legislation have gone on to be indicted for criminal activities, there is no evidence he knew anything about it. Our office went to extremes to find incriminating evidence. This is probably why he isn't very fond of us. However, he is as he appears—a very smart, honest lobbyist."

The director read the next file about Clara. "Mrs. Clara Ann Pinckney Witherspoon. Born July tenth, 1948, in San Diego. Graduated from the community college twenty-three years later and went to work at the public library. She married Henry Witherspoon two years later. He died of cancer six years ago. Agents Marlin and McFearson questioned her at length, so it's safe to assume she is not overly fond of us, as well." The director paused.

"Last but certainly not least is the character calling himself George Washington. First known appearance was on a beach on the coast of Southern California in the company of Jeff Thompson. Washington's appearance suggests he is a senior citizen, but it is apparent he possesses martial skills and is quite adept at defending himself. He thwarted two criminal attacks—one of which Terrance George perpetrated. As you already know, he bested Agents Hancock and McFearson in an unwarranted arrest attempt. Due to his rising popularity, I believe he possesses charismatic qualities only achieved after years of public speaking.

"Other than defending himself or someone in need, his actions show he has an interest in promoting the public good. The most important thing to remember is he won't back down if he believes his cause is just.

"I've been in contact with Police Chief Adams in San Diego, and I believe it's because of those qualities he made him an honorary police officer for his actions in stopping criminal activity. Chief Adams also said he was instrumental in helping Agent Hancock recover from his mental stress illness."

President Saunders shook his head. "So now you're telling me two people we pissed off beyond measure and a yet-to-be-identified man who seems in line for sainthood are trying to bring perhaps a couple thousand of their friends to come speak to me. Is that it, Director Butler?"

"At this point, yes, Mr. President," replied Butler.

"I'm hoping you have a recommendation, Director," Saunders said cautiously.

"I do," Butler replied. "Allow him to make his journey. There is nothing in his behavior that would suggest he means you or the country any harm, and he is one of the most interesting people we've ever encountered. I think whatever he has to say will be equally interesting. There might also be an opportunity to capitalize on his popularity."

"What you're saying makes sense," the president admitted, "but I'm accustomed to having more information than this."

"I'm certain the Secret Service and local law enforcement will be able to handle the arrival of a couple thousand people," the director said confidently.

CHAPTER 25

The next venue was Albuquerque, New Mexico. The trio of vehicles pulled up, and everyone knew exactly what to do. This indoor theater could hold five thousand if necessary. Ticket prices were just enough to cover the venue, and many took advantage of the low expense.

George took the stage as he had done the first time and began his discourse. "Citizens of Albuquerque, thank you for your attendance this evening. By now, most are aware of my desire to speak to the president once we arrive at the capital. In recompense for your support and the good tidings I have experienced here in your fair city, I will offer you a partial chronicle of my personal history that cannot be found in the history books.

"At the time of my youth," George proceeded, "in what is now Virginia, the region was merely a British colony. My father's trade was that of a tobacco plantation owner."

George's posture changed. His walk brought him to center stage, and for the first time, George broke eye contact with the audience. He stood there holding his hat with both hands, and his eyes gazed at the floor. "As many already know, my father owned many slaves."

A wave of jeers and unkind slurs emanated from the audience, and George let this display of anger continue for a couple of minutes. During that time, he just stood there and took it, and then something happened that has probably never happened on a stage anywhere: suddenly, George rebuked the audience.

In an extremely loud, commanding voice, he said, "How dare you chastise me for my father's actions! Have this nation's citizens become so fearful and cowardly that the mere mention of impropriety causes them to lash out in anger without knowing the full facts of the matter?"

There was an instant and absolute silence in a room with nearly five thousand people.

George broke the silence. "I will ask this of all before me. Allow me to continue my chronicle unimpeded by hateful words. At its conclusion, I will accept your judgment of those actions I am solely responsible for." The audience seemed to regain some of its composure, so George continued. "I am very much aware of this country's attitude concerning slavery and all the villainy associated with it. I would ask you to believe me when I say this assemblage is not the first group of people to feel this way."

George had their undivided attention again, so he continued his walk back and forth across the front of the stage. His mannerisms carried a dire attitude. There was no doubt he wanted the audience to understand his tale. "'Tis true what the historical accounts say," George said. "Much cruelty and bloodshed arose among those who owned slaves at that time. Even as a young boy, I was not blind to the suffering wrought upon the fieldworkers. Though the home I lived in was grand in design, 'twas not distant enough from the slave quarters that I could not hear the wailing and crying of those abused through the night.

"I inquired of my father on numerous occasions about the disciplining of the workers. It is a very natural thing for a son to believe everything his father says unconditionally, and I was no exception when my father told me it was necessary to be deliberately cruel to maintain order. I believed him until I met one man who changed my thoughts concerning slavery, Mr. Frederick Douglass.

"While I was still a young man, a number of slaves were bought and sold on my father's estate. A particular instance occurred one evening when a wagon arrived from

Charleston bearing a solitary slave purchase. The man was taken to temporary quarters and incarcerated there.

"Because I had no stomach for the mistreatment of our workers, my father believed me weak and unworthy of the tobacco empire he sought to achieve. He took every opportunity to compel me into undesirable circumstances with the workers. He hoped I would one day follow in his footsteps.

"On the eve of Mr. Douglass's arrival, Father instructed me to go to the quarters where Douglass had been locked up and give him his ration of food and the introductory speech every new acquisition received. I unlocked the door to the shed, and as I entered, I saw a black man in tattered clothes chained to the wall in irons. From the amount of blood crusted to his face and the swollen bruises on his cheeks and jaw, I could tell our taskmaster had already been there to welcome him.

"I unlocked one of the manacles so he could eat, and I set the dish on the floor in front of him. He looked withered and fatigued. 'Twas an enormous effort for him to reach down to grasp the food.

"I sat upon a crate against the front wall of the shed and began the lecture as my father had instructed me. 'You are here to work, slave! If you work well, then you need not fear me. If you work poorly, then the lash will not be spared! Do you understand me, slave?'

"After he managed to swallow a handful of food, he looked me in the eyes with his head tilted toward the ground. In a barely audible voice, he whispered, 'Name.'

"'Twas not the response I expected. I asked, 'What do you mean? Is it your name or my name you wish to convey? Surely you do not expect introductions.'

"'Young sir,' Douglass began, 'if you would have me work, then that is what I will do. If you wish to lay your lash upon me, then do so. I would ask only to know who it is I have to thank.' Douglass was out of breath at that point.

"My parents had reared me to be mannerly at all times, so I instinctively said, 'I am George, son of Augustine Washington, your owner.'

"'Well then, Master George, I am Frederick Douglass, picker of tobacco and cotton and currently slave to your father.'

"This made me angry, and I said, 'Do you mock me, Douglass?'

"'Not at all,' he replied. 'I am simply trying to render you as much respect as I can under present circumstances.'

"'You do not speak as the other slaves do. Why is that?' I asked.

"'My last master was a man of some importance, and I traveled extensively in his company,' Douglass explained.

'During our last journey together, he lost my services in a game of chance. Then I found myself in an auction house in Charleston, where your father's agent purchased me.'

"Douglass's strength was leaving him again. I found his story intriguing, so after a period of silence, I asked him to continue. Over the next several hours, Douglass related to me all his travels that brought him to my father's estate. In the midst of this, I continued to bring him food and drink.

"When his tales were at an end, I replaced the manacle upon his wrist and returned to my bedchamber, for the hour was late. I had only been asleep a few hours when the screams of a man having the lash repeatedly applied to him woke me.

"I hastened from my bed to find Father and the taskmaster lashing Douglass where he was chained to the wall. I grabbed my father by the arm and bade him to cease whipping Douglass, but he cast me to the ground. He said, 'I have always believed one day you would inherit all I have and conduct the affairs of business appropriately. I see now I was wrong!'

"'Tis my belief Douglass's kindness of speech and courteous manner offended Father, because the next day Douglass was taken back to Charleston to be sold again."

Yet another silence gripped the crowd, and the air was heavy with thoughtful contemplation.

"Gentlemen and ladies of the audience, what is missing from the history books and what I now impart to you is this:

after my father's death, I did, in fact, gain everything my father possessed. There were over sixty slaves on the estate at that time, and under my rule every slave was treated with kindness, courtesy, and respect. They were treated as family members with all the privileges accorded to my family.

"My industry flourished and became the envy of other plantation owners. However, I came under sharp criticism by the community when the methods by which I conducted my home affairs became public knowledge.

"I am not one who immediately bows to social convention when it conflicts with what I know is true and proper, for I can never run far enough or fast enough to escape my own conscience. No matter where I go, I am always there.

"As my influence grew, 'twas not enough for me to simply treat my slaves better. I knew a revolution from Britain was inevitable, and I knew any country that would be spawned from such a great conflict would only survive the test of time if all men were free and able to defend it together.

"It became known to me that another plantation owner—someone known as Thomas Jefferson—had a similar way of regarding his slaves. After the passage of time and both our ascensions to political prominence, we sought others who felt as we did and began an abolitionist movement. We believed all slavery could be dispelled at a future time."

George paused for a moment and listened to the murmurings of the audience. Then he continued. "I have reviewed in great detail this nation's history, and I have discovered the same slave owners and abolitionist families that I and others originally recruited for the movement did indeed continue their antislavery efforts. President Abraham Lincoln had the courage and strength of character to strike the final blow to end slavery forever!"

George's crescendo at the end of his last statement brought a standing ovation from all in attendance. George bowed in his most gentlemanly way in gratitude to the audience. When the applause diminished, he went on.

"Of all former presidents, I believe President Lincoln and I would have been kindred spirits had I known him. I am certain he knew, just as I knew, the price of abolishing slavery would be high, but the benefits of its elimination would be even higher."

George concluded his speech. "I would caution each and every person within the sound of my voice not to rush to judgment when facing the unknown or circumstances that do not seem to fit your preconceptions and expectations. Use your eyes to see and your minds to discern. Then act with your heart and conscience, and this nation can be great once again."

CHAPTER 26

The next stop for the trio was Amarillo, Texas. Jeff thought it would be enjoyable to have a campout along the way. The sun was setting on the horizon when they neared the halfway point to their destination, so they found an empty stretch of highway to pull off the road a bit and set some chairs out to have a fire.

From one of the box trucks, an armchair with very plush upholstery was retrieved for Clara to sit in. Jeff, George, and the three security guards/drivers were relegated to camping chairs. The fire was warm, and the sun was casting beautiful hues of red and blue across the desert landscape.

Clara was sitting beside George, and she remarked, "I have seen thousands of desert sunsets in library books, but there is no comparison to seeing the actual thing before your eyes."

"Indeed, Clara," George replied. "'Tis a glorious sight to behold. In my travels, I have ventured no farther than the

Mississippi River. I am fortunate to have you to share this experience with."

Jeff and the other three men excused themselves to attend to supper. They went to the back of the first truck to set up the grill. Clara sat there quietly for a moment.

"How long has it been since you've seen Martha?"

Without missing a beat, George replied instinctively. "It has been more than four months since I have gazed upon her countenance."

At that moment, George knew he had slipped up, and Clara became certain of her suspicions. George's face began to turn an unusual shade of crimson, and for the first time since they met, George had difficulty saying what was on his mind. After a few stutters and stammers, he simply gave up trying.

Clara reached over and laid her hand atop his. She grinned a bit and said, "Why, George Washington, I do believe you're blushing!"

George found it impossible to say anything. Clara patted his hand. "I've known from the beginning, George. It would be impossible to work at a library for fifty years and not know a famous historical figure such as yourself intimately."

"You are a remarkable woman, Clara," George said.

"I will not dispute that statement," declared Clara.

For George, it seemed as though a tremendous burden had been lifted from his shoulders. "Would you care for a beverage, Clara?" he asked.

"Some tea would do nicely, George. Thank you," Clara replied.

George stood and went to the RV. Once inside, he started preparations for some tea. From somewhere in the front of the vehicle, George heard a voice.

"George…hey, George. You there? Say something if you can hear me."

George looked around the two front seats and the dashboard. Then he replied, "Yes, I can hear you. To whom am I speaking?"

"George, this is Phil. I'm speaking to you through the navigation system in the RV. I'm here with Chief Adams."

"Yeah, George. I'm here, too. I don't know how, but I am," the chief said.

"Phil, Bob, 'tis certainly good to hear from you. How may I be of service?" George asked.

Phil answered, "First, it is very important you get Jeff and have him open his laptop right away."

"Very well, gentlemen. I will return in a moment."

A minute later, George and Jeff returned, and Jeff retrieved his laptop from the RV's dash. When he opened it, he saw an image of Phil and Bob with their faces filling the screen like two teenagers making a covert midnight Skype call. Jeff and George had their faces equally close to the screen.

"What's going on, fellas?" Jeff asked.

"Listen, Jeff, you don't have a lot of time," Phil said. "I've got a FLIR satellite view of your current position. There are six heavily armed men advancing on you from the south and what looks like one coming down from the north along the road on foot. At their current speeds, they should reach your encampment in about fifteen minutes. Both groups have vehicles parked about a quarter mile away. I'm detecting night-vision emissions, so they can see in the dark."

Then an infrared real-time image replaced Phil and Bob. Sure enough, six red dots were coming up from the south and one from the north.

"Any minute, NASA is going to realize the Hubble isn't pointed out into deep space anymore, so this image might not last. Whatever you're going to do, get cracking."

George and Jeff went to where Clara was sitting and called the guards over. Each man dropped to one knee around Clara.

Jeff said, "George, you're the military strategist of our group. What's the plan?"

George pointed to one of the security guards. "You, sir, take Clara a hundred yards east under as much cover as you can find. Circle to the south, and commandeer the scoundrels' car. Then drive Clara and yourself to safety. Go now!"

Clara didn't even have time to object. The guard had her out of sight in a moment.

"You other men," George continued, "find cover. As targets of opportunity arise, you can deal with them as you see fit. Apparently they can see in the dark, so conceal yourselves accordingly. Jeff, you and I will sit here by the fire and see what happens."

"We're gonna do what?" Jeff exclaimed.

"Jeffery, calm yourself. We are outnumbered and barely armed. There is no victory in direct combat this night. Our best defense now is the application of guile."

Jeff and George sat there quietly, and Jeff kept tabs on the interlopers with his laptop. He could see three of the six coming from the south taking positions about forty yards out in a semicircle around the desert side of the encampment. The other three continued on a straight line to the campfire. When they reached the vehicles, one stopped at the front of the second truck. Another stopped at the back of the RV, and the last one continued forward until firelight bathed him. The fellow in the north was just loitering at the road.

"Well, the great and mighty G. Dub himself! I bet you never thought you'd see me again."

"As I recall," George said politely, "we were not formally introduced. I know you were quite busy at the time trying to make off with my…how did you put it? My bitch of a girlfriend. 'Tis an unseemly reference, to be sure."

"Speaking of her, is she around? I'd like to kill her after I finish with you and the geek."

"Jeffery, what is a geek?" George asked in an extremely calm manner.

Nervously, Jeff answered, "It's a person who likes to spend a lot of time on computers."

"Ah. Thank you, Jeffery," George said smoothly.

As George and Terrance were speaking, Jeff noticed that the red dot from the north had begun to move toward the three dots positioned out in the desert scrub. After a moment or two, the red dot that was in motion merged briefly with one of the stationary dots. Then the red dot moved off and left behind a blue dot that gradually disappeared. The second stationary dot merged and then disappeared in the same way as the first. As the third dot was about to suffer the same fate, Jeff saw another red dot appear from nowhere and merge with the one in front of the second truck. Yet another appeared mysteriously and merged with the one behind the RV.

There were only three dots left that weren't at the fire, and they just stood there waiting.

"Terrance—" George started.

"My name is King George, you piece of shit old man!" Terrance shouted.

George continued unperturbed. "Did you look into any historical references before you claimed ownership of that name?"

Terrance stepped forward and stood directly in front of where George was sitting. He reached down and grabbed George by the shirt. "No. Is there something about my name I should know?"

George replied, "Two hundred thirty eight years ago, the original King George found fault with me. In the end, 'twas necessary for me to kick not only his ass but all his minions' asses as well. I hope I used that term correctly. You have left me with no alternative but to do the same to you."

With that, George brought his boot up squarely into Terrance's groin, and the big man howled like a banshee. George tilted backward in his chair until it went over all the way. He continued his roll and came back to a standing position. Jeff bolted to the far side of the fire and watched. He was looking for a means to help George.

Terrance recovered and began to pursue George. George tried to back away to gain more distance and fighting room, but for a big man, Terrance was quick. In the firelight, Iustitia made an appearance like a laser beam.

George ducked, spun, and sidestepped Terrance for what seemed like hours. Every turn or change of position George made brought a corresponding blow to some portion of Terrance's body. Massive strikes from George's instrument of justice peppered the criminal.

The tide of the battle had driven the two combatants into the road, and there in the open, the engagement was to be decided. George was beginning to tire. All his skirmishes thus far had been extremely brief, and Terrance had youth on his side.

George's avoidance of Terrance's wild blows didn't last. Terrance managed to land a tremendous blow to George's right cheek. It sent him sailing through the air to land on the edge of the road.

Terrance had expended a lot of energy during the fight, so he shuffled over to where George lay and withdrew a pistol from his jacket. He pointed it right at George. In the blink of an eye, the big man was cart wheeling through the air ten feet off the ground. The roar of an SUV could be heard as it continued on into the distance.

Terrance landed on his head and cleanly snapped his neck. Jeff ran over to George, who was still shaking off the impact to his face.

Jeff knelt at his side, and George said, "Did you best him, Jeffery?"

"It wasn't me." Jeff looked bewildered.

The two security guards showed up. One said, "We saw you the whole time, George, but we didn't know any way to help that wouldn't have screwed up that fancy ballet you were doing with your sword."

Jeff helped George to his feet, and around that time the SUV that had mowed down Terrance returned. It drove slowly as it approached. The tinted windows obscured the driver's face. Jeff noticed that the front of the vehicle was caved in severely, and only one headlight was intact.

The SUV came to a stop beside Terrance's lifeless body. The door opened, and the driver stepped out and stood close to Terrance's head. The driver pointed a wrinkled index finger at him and yelled, "Don't fuck with a librarian!"

George limped over to Clara and wrapped his arms around her. The third security guard showed up out of breath. He told George that as he was dispatching the getaway driver, Clara hopped in the SUV and took off.

"Why, Clara, that was perfectly naughty," George mused.

"That is how I meant it," Clara said stubbornly.

The entire group went back to the fire, and Jeff picked up his laptop. Phil's image returned, and Jeff reported that everyone was all right except for the bad guys.

Phil said, "Before NASA stole the Hubble back, I watched the battle, and there is still one bad guy left. The last I saw, he was standing in front of the RV watching George and Terrance."

All eyes turned to the front of the RV, and a familiar voice came booming from the shadows.

"Don't you be callin' me a bad guy, Phil. You don't even know me at all!"

Agent McFearson joined them at the fire. "Chief Adams, you still there, me fine fellow?" Dan asked.

"Yes, I'm still here," came the chief's voice.

"You and Phil be gettin' on OK?" asked Dan.

"Sure are. Haven't a clue about all his tech stuff, but we seem to work well together," he replied.

"Then would you be so kind as to get the local fellas out here to clean up this mess? The bodies of these seven arseholes be stinkin' up the desert. You might wanna get a hold of the director at the Department of Homeland Security and fill him in. He'll have a shite fit, no doubt."

CHAPTER 27

Late in the afternoon of the following day, George, Jeff, and Clara were sitting at a diner in Amarillo next to the theatre and reviewing the events of the past evening.

Jeff turned to George. "As you and Terrance were talking, I was the only one who could see what was happening. You had no idea his other minions had been taken out. Yet you still struck at Terrance. Weren't you concerned his buddies would gang up on you or shoot you from a hidden position?"

"My dear Jeffery," George explained, "in any conflict one might find oneself involved with, the person standing the closest is always the most imminent threat. I ignored the other villains and dealt with the one at hand. Once that threat was discharged, then I moved to the next one. There is little to be gained by concerning oneself with all assailants at once."

Jeff took a few sips of his coffee. "While Clara and I were giving our statements to the police, you and Agent McFearson seemed to have a very lengthy conversation. What did he have to say?"

"He cautioned me to be ever vigilant in my travels to the capital. The person or persons who contracted Terrance and his henchmen are still unknown and liable to strike again," George replied. "Dan is still at odds between his desire to gain retribution for the injuries he sustained in our first engagement and his wish to find the truth of these circumstances that keep arising. As we spoke last evening, I could see his anger with me directly behind his eyes."

"I don't understand how he can be that way. Surely by now he must know you are no threat to anyone or at least anyone who isn't trying to hurt us."

"'Tis my belief Dan's heart knows the truth of my intentions, but his head continues to be an obstacle," George stated firmly. "I also spoke with Phil and Bob at length. They are going to continue to look into Terrance's associates and financial dealings to see if there are any demons that might be brought into the light."

Since the events of the previous evening had concluded, Clara had not said a lot about them. Through the course of the meal they were finishing, she seemed lost in thought.

As Jeff and George discussed the details of that evening's speech, George noticed a profound sadness beginning to show on Clara's face. After a while, Jeff excused himself to attend to a few matters at the theatre. This left George and Clara at the booth alone.

George reached over and took Clara's hand. "Trepidation does not belong on a face as kindly as yours, Clara," he said softly. "What preys upon your mind?"

Clara sat there staring at her plate, and George noticed her lower lip quivering a bit. Then she uttered a sentence. "I've never killed anyone before."

The sadness on her face began to deepen.

"Clara," George said solemnly, "I would ask that you listen closely to what I have to say. Do you believe me to be a monster or one who enjoys the harming of others?"

Clara shook her head.

"You know my history better than almost anyone. I have killed in single combat hundreds of times, and orders I have given have caused the deaths of thousands of patriots. I have read there is a time and season for everything—for every activity under the heavens. I believe there were no truer words ever spoken.

"There is a comfort to be gained when the truth of this statement is realized. The guilt and regret associated with the killing of another are never truly dispelled, but they do become a bit easier to live with.

"In the case of the criminals, the choices they made put them in positions that caused their demises. Their behavior is that of mice or rats or any sort of vermin. They cause pestilence and are detriments to society.

"You, Clara, did an extremely hard and necessary thing. You took responsibility for my safety and put yourself at risk. Twice. For those actions I will be indebted to you for all my days. The undesirable feelings you are currently experiencing will never go away, but I can say with absolute certainty they will become easier to live with."

Clara's mood seemed to lighten a bit, and George said, "Let us retire to the motor home. I am sure Jeffery can manage things until speech time."

George and Clara made their way back to the theater and the private parking area that contained the trucks and RV. The pair conversed quietly as they walked. It was a beautiful day in Amarillo, and it seemed the events of last night were far away.

As they approached, two men dressed in black suits and dark sunglasses stepped in front of the RV door. Instantly, Iustitia was brought forth in defense of George and Clara.

Then the man carrying a briefcase said, "Mr. Washington, please stand down. We are unarmed and have a message for you."

George said, "Recent events have compromised my ability to trust strange persons. Open the fronts of your coats, if you please, so I can know for certain."

The briefcase was set down, and both men opened their jackets wide. All was as they said.

"Clara," George urged, "please go in the theater and get Jeffery and our security friends. Have them wait out here until my dealings with these two individuals conclude. They will need to be escorted off the premises shortly."

Clara did as George asked, and the three men entered the RV for a conference. The two men sat at the dining table, where George indicated with a gesture. He then pushed a button on the wall that opened the blinds to the large picture window in that area of the RV.

One of the men asked, "Mr. Washington, would you please close that blind? This is a private message just for you."

"Gentlemen," George began, "I have grown weary of all the subterfuge that has been inflicted upon me since my arrival. My tolerance is at an end. Please deliver your message or depart. 'Tis your choice."

The two men looked at each other briefly. The one with the briefcase put it on the table and opened it. He seemed to work a keyboard. Then he turned it around so George could see the contents, and it appeared to be a communications device with a view screen. The great seal of the United States of America was on the screen for a moment. Then the face of a well-dressed black man replaced it.

"Good day to you, President Saunders," George said. "I knew at some point I would capture your attention. What can I do for you this day?"

"Well, Mr. Washington," the president began, "you can start by telling me who you really are and what you're really up to with all this notoriety you're accumulating."

"Mr. President, I am exactly and precisely who I claim to be. Have you been involved with so many lies, falsehoods, and half-truths your mind has closed to all but your preconceptions?" George asked.

"You expect me to believe you are the George Washington who was the first president of the United States?" Saunders asked.

"I am sensing, Mr. President, that no matter what I have to say, you will take me for a liar and scoundrel. I have made my identity known and my intentions clear. If you are so insecure and fearful you will not have an open dialogue with me in a public forum, then this nation and its leadership have most assuredly fallen from grace, and matters are indeed much worse than I believed."

"Why is it necessary for you to bring a large group of people to Washington?" the president asked.

"Would you have allowed an audience with me if I had arrived at the White House alone and claimed to be George Washington?" George inquired. "When I occupied that position, common citizens were received cordially to speak with me. My, how times have changed." George continued. "What do you have to fear, Mr. President? I bring with me this nation's citizenry, many of whom, no doubt, voted for you. They have troubles and concerns they wish to make known. Would you deny them their voices?

"I do not desire your office. I held it for two terms, which is proper. I do not desire to overthrow this government, for 'tis a great one when its leaders allow it to be. I do not desire armed conflict, for we are all Americans deserving of the rights and privileges the Constitution guarantees. My sole purpose is as it's always been—to bring accountability back to this country's citizens and to remind you and those in Washington the people of this country do have voices, and they will not be ignored."

President Saunders sat on his side of the screen agape. No one had ever spoken to him in such a commanding tone. Before the president could say another word, George continued.

"I am fully aware there are threats to this nation of which I am currently oblivious. I will concede that point to you, Mr. President. I will allow one of your agents at this table to remain with my group and monitor our activities. He may report to you in whatever fashion he sees fit. You will see my cause is just and my intentions are honorable, but if he interferes with our efforts, I will expel him personally. If he tries to harm me or any of my friends and associates, he will be counted among the lot we left in the desert.

"In the meantime, Mr. President, I suggest you contact Mr. Thompson to coordinate our arrival six weeks hence. We are, after all, bringing a number of guests with us."

One of the agents put his hand to his earpiece and acknowledged his orders. The other agent closed the briefcase and departed.

George asked the remaining man, "How shall I address you, sir?"

"I am Agent Rodger Sherman of the Secret Service," the man replied. "You may address me as Agent Sherman."

"Very well, Agent Sherman; welcome to our company. I ask that through the course of your stay with us, if you perceive anything at all that might be construed as a threat to this nation or the president, you inform me immediately so we can deal with it together. Does that sound like an equitable arrangement, Agent Sherman?"

"It does," the agent replied.

"Then please follow me," George asked politely.

The two men exited the RV, and as requested, Jeff and the three security guards were there waiting for him.

George stated bluntly, "This is Agent Sherman of the Secret Service. I've asked that he remain with us to address any security issues that might manifest as we journey. Jeffery, I ask you to include Agent Sherman in all your preparations for our arrival. I realize the amount of discomfort you're feeling concerning this, but I want the people in the capital to welcome us. That will not happen if they feel they are being invaded. If you two gentlemen reach an impasse, bring your concerns to me, and we will rectify it together. Please make the appropriate accommodations for him."

CHAPTER 28

Jeff and company did as George asked. That evening in Amarillo, Agent Sherman could be seen periodically with his hand on his earpiece, talking to some unknown person.

George finished his speech to fervent applause and ovations from the crowd. The same was true in Oklahoma City, Tulsa, St. Louis, and Indianapolis.

Between George, Jeff, and Agent Sherman, they hammered out an accord by which George and the people he convinced to join him could enter the capital and speak to the president. Once the White House acknowledged the meeting, the national press and TV networks began to take serious notice of George. They clambered for every scrap of information they could get their hands on.

Phil was extremely helpful with setting up a website. Those who wished to support George could register and download the conditions of their participation.

A rallying point was established just outside Centreville, Virginia, at a farm with two hundred acres of open land. Camping accommodations would be made available to participants. Over the course of two days, people would gather there, and then at the appointed time, George would lead them on a march to the capital.

As they left the rally point, the Secret Service would search individuals for firearms. Violators would be subject to arrest. Agents would take positions along the route, marching among the citizens in disguise. George supported the Secret Service in this matter and made all in attendance aware. Once in the capital, the general public would gather on the grounds of the National Mall to witness this event. At its conclusion, whatever it might be, those in attendance would simply leave the way they came.

In Canton, Ohio, George stood atop the steps of the McKinley Monument and delivered yet another stirring speech.

"In my studies of this nation's history since the time of my presidency," he began, "only four presidents have been lost to assassins' bullets: Abraham Lincoln, James Garfield, William McKinley, and John F. Kennedy. Knowing them only from the history they left behind, 'tis my belief they too had aspirations for the continuance of our nation, but the forces of evil and cowards' acts cut short their efforts.

"Threats against this country and its leaders have increased by an order of magnitude since its beginnings. It is not the pressure from other nations that occupies my thoughts. It is those whom we elect to perform functions in the government's continuation and who instead use their positions to create dynasties and empires for themselves or for others at the expense of the general population.

"This is at the very heart of the matter that will bring me to Washington for a reckoning of accountability. Those of you who choose to join me will add your voices to those of all the people who have toiled and strained under the yoke of a conflicted Congress and of judicial and executive branches whose abilities to work as one to forward the nation's interests are called into question.

"At what point was it decided two political parties could supply the best people to oversee our country? In every place I have traveled since my return, I have noticed an overabundance of choices for the people of this nation.

"The marketplaces I have visited never offer just two kinds of bread, meat, or spirits. Sellers of personal conveyances have considerably more than two kinds of transports for purchase.

"My friend Mr. Thompson has shown me that in the media, the majority of advertisements are for either Democrats or Republicans. The two dominant parties might be suppressing other parties. I am uncertain. I do know Americans favor many choices, and social convention would suggest two choices are insufficient."

After George finished his speech and thrilled all who were there, he returned to the RV for a well-deserved dining experience with Clara. Halfway through the meal, Agent Sherman knocked on the door, and Clara answered it. The agent entered and set another briefcase before George. Sherman activated the view screen, and the president appeared.

"Good evening, Mr. President," George said. "What can I do for you this evening?"

"I just wanted to let you know all the preparations for your arrival are complete on our side. There is an open-air table set up in front of the Capitol building, and all the media cameras will be documenting our discussion from a distance."

"Thank you, Mr. President. 'Tis wonderful news. The tenor of your voice suggests your misgivings about this event are not quite as dubious as they once were," George said.

"I have to admit, Mr. Washington, the reports I've been getting from Agent Sherman and the GOP polls seem to corroborate what you have been saying all along. You're only interested in raising awareness. I'm still not comfortable having my administration under the microscope like this, but if there are better ways of doing things, then I would very much like to hear them."

George offered, "You might find it interesting, Mr. President, but from my perspective, it has been only eight years since I chose the ground the Capitol now sits upon and six years since I laid the cornerstone at its massive base in an extremely auspicious ceremony. I do wish the moment could have been saved in the fashion in which modern history is recorded."

"I am still having a lot of difficulty accepting that you are the original George Washington. That idea defies everything I believe to be true," Saunders admitted.

"Would you accept my identity if I provided you with irrefutable proof from a source you already have in your possession—no matter how strange or unseemly it might be?" asked George.

"It would have to be truly irrefutable. If so, then yes. I would," Saunders said wholeheartedly.

"Then I ask you to have Agents Marlin and McFearson join us at the table at the capital. Before our dialogue begins, I will divulge the whereabouts of this evidence, and they can retrieve it. If it is as irrefutable as I say, then we will continue our discussion as scheduled."

"You have my curiosity piqued, Mr. Washington, so I will agree to your terms," the president said.

"Very well. If something changes between now and the time I arrive, please contact me again, Mr. President. Good evening to you," George said.

"And to you, Mr. Washington," Saunders replied.

Agent Sherman closed the briefcase, and George thanked him for his delivery of the message. Then the agent departed.

CHAPTER 29

By the time George and his company reached the rallying point, a large number of vehicles had already arrived. The security and help was engaged to ensure the orderly arrangement of the camping areas were doing a superb job. As the people arrived, they settled in a well-organized fashion.

On the evening of the second day, George received a visitor. While George and Clara were sitting at a picnic table outside the RV, Jeff approached with George's favorite hairdresser, Thom, in tow.

"Georgie! It's glorious to see you again," Thom said. He ran up to George and hugged him from behind. "I've watched you on TV, and you are looking so dapper in your fabulous retro uniforms."

After his embrace, Thom took a seat beside Jeff, across from George and Clara.

George introduced Thom to Clara. "Clara, this is my good friend and master barber, Thom. Thom, this is my friend and traveling companion, Mrs. Clara Witherspoon."

"Why, Georgie, when you were sitting in my salon, you never mentioned you had such a lovely lady friend. I had to learn all about her secondhand from Jeffrey. You two look so darling together. It's as if Norman Rockwell just set you both on a canvas for all to admire!"

Thom was at the beginning of another rolling string of dialogue, but before he could gain momentum, George interrupted. "Master Thom, please be at ease. I'm sure your arrival here is fraught with purpose and design. I hope you would share it with me at some point."

Thom looked at Jeff. "You haven't told him yet?" Thom said.

"No, I haven't," Jeff replied. "I thought I would let you do the honors."

"Well, Georgie, you are in for a real treat! Jeff and I have planned that tomorrow morning I am going to give you and Ms. Clara simply fabulous hairstyles befitting the retro style that seems to appeal to you and the grandeur of the momentous occasion that's about to unfold. Jeffery has gone to great lengths to secure colonial-style clothes for you to wear. George, you have a military dress uniform, and Ms. Clara has a formal ball gown with all the lace and trimmings. When the time comes for you to lead all your friends to the capital, you and Ms. Clara will be driven in a horse-drawn open-air coach. Strung out behind you will be everyone you asked to join you. I don't know how you can stand all this excitement. I would've already had to be sedated to keep from going crazy!"

"'Tis an extraordinary time, to be sure, Thom," George stated. "Many people have worked hard to see this day, and I do thank you and Jeffery for your efforts."

True to his word, Thom had George and Clara's hair looking remarkably historical, and their period clothes gave all who witnessed them a brief glimpse into the nation's colonial beginnings.

The Secret Service, as well as other federal agents, did a wonderful job of organizing the civilians in eight columns of twenty people long. This created squads of 160 people. George and Clara began the slow carriage ride to the capital, and each squad of citizens fell in behind them.

As they traveled, Clara remarked, "I am having a hard time believing the reality of what's happening. This feels as if some sort of Cinderella story is at work here."

"What is a Cinderella story?" George asked.

"It's a story about a young woman whose stepmother and sisters mistreat her, and through the efforts of her fairy godmother, she attends a royal ball and falls in love with the prince. As the magic begins to fade, she leaves him behind. All that remains is one of the glass slippers she was wearing. The prince uses the slipper to identify the woman in the village, and they live happily ever after."

"I can assure you, Clara, this is indeed happening." George beamed. "I do recall a French story entitled *Cendrillon, ou la Petite Pantoufle de Verre,* or *The Little Glass Slipper.* 'Twas a story I cherished from my childhood."

As George and Clara reminisced about days past, they could hear the sound of the squad leaders calling cadence and the steady beat of thousands of feet hitting the road. People were lining the road. It was sporadic at first but became more frequent the closer they came to the capital.

The massive group of citizens marched through Fairfax, Falls Church, and Arlington on their way to the Capitol building and the National Mall.

As the carriage with George and Clara was preparing to cross the Potomac River, Agent Sherman walked up to the side of the carriage and asked permission to board it. George consented, and the Agent took a seat opposite George. Once again, he opened a communications briefcase so George could talk to the president.

"Good afternoon, Mr. President," George greeted. "We will be arriving within the hour. I am looking forward to meeting you in person."

President Saunders replied, "I thought you'd like to know that the latest tally of the folk marching behind you is one point fifteen million people. The Secret Service has only arrested twelve people for weapons violations, so it appears almost everyone is following the rules. I thought there would be a lot more trouble than this."

"The evening is far from over, Mr. President," George cautioned. "I ask that in addition to yourself and the vice president attending your side of the table, you have two of your most trusted Secret Service agents, as well. I believe we will both have need of their services."

"Expecting some trouble, Mr. Washington?" the president asked.

"Nothing that two of your finest agents could not deal with if necessary," George replied.

"Very well, Mr. Washington," Saunders said. "They will be standing by. See you shortly."

George thanked Agent Sherman. The agent closed the communications case and departed.

The National Mall, as well as the Lincoln Memorial, finally came into view. All the open areas from the river to the steps of the Capitol building were marked off in such a way that a squad of citizens would fit perfectly in each lot. The aisles were left open so emergency services could get to anyone who needed them.

Monitors and speakers were set up the entire length of the Mall, so no matter where one stood, there was a clear view of the proceedings. By the time the carriage containing George and Clara reached the foot of the steps at the Capitol building, the sun was beginning its descent toward the horizon.

A staging area was set up at the top of the steps, so George and Clara could rest before the president's arrival. It took an additional hour and a half for the remainder of the civilians to get in their places. Counting those who marched and those who simply showed up in Washington, it was estimated there were a full two million people in attendance for the evening's forum. Jeff joined George just as the president arrived. Clara stayed at the staging area to view the proceedings. Then Jeff and George took their places at the opposite side of the table from the president and his company.

On the president's side were the vice president and Agents Marlin and McFearson. Standing directly behind them were the two Secret Service agents George had asked for. The sun was rapidly approaching the horizon, and the shadow from the Washington Monument was pointing directly at George.

CHAPTER 30

The president began. "Gentlemen, good evening. I'd like to introduce you to the person who helps me hold things together, Vice President John Dayton. John, these are the men you have no doubt heard so much about—Mr. Jeffery Thompson and Mr. George Washington."

John replied, "I'm honored to finally meet both of you. I have been following closely your journey to the capital, and I must say your determination has earned the respect of many here in Washington and all over the country."

Agents Marlin and McFearson sat at the end of the table, where they could see everyone. Agent Marlin had his gaze fixed on George. The resentment and loathing he had for George was beaming from his eyes like a projected energy weapon. George had forever stained Dirk's career, and as George listened to Vice President Dayton, he could feel Dirk's eyes boring a hole through his skull. When George threw a glance in Dirk's direction, he realized he had cost Agent Marlin considerably more than was generally known.

Agent McFearson was carefully watching everything. He was regarding everyone at the table suspiciously, and with the addition of the two Secret Service agents, he became even more uneasy.

After all the pleasantries were exchanged, President Saunders said, "Before we get into the meat and potatoes of your visit, we have a couple agreements to discharge, don't we?"

"We do indeed," George agreed. "As you know, there have been a great many forces working against me since my journey began, and with monumental efforts on the parts of some dear and gracious friends, I now know the truth of the darkness that seems to haunt me. Jeffery, if you please."

Jeff put his laptop on the table and opened it so the president could see. The crest of the Department of Homeland Security showed for a brief moment. Then all the monitors in the Mall switched to split screen. One half had the television coverage broadcast. The other half showed a view of the laptop screen.

The crest dissolved into an image of Agent Hancock. "President Saunders, Vice President Dayton, good evening. I have information to report that will shed light on the attacks on Mr. Washington but also on incidents involving other federal agents."

"Proceed," Saunders said nervously.

"After the attack on Mr. Washington and his party in the desert outside Amarillo, Police Chief Adams and I began a very long and drawn-out search into the financial background of the now-deceased Terrance Rutherford George and all his criminal associates. Two weeks before the assault, one hundred thousand dollars was deposited into an offshore account of one of Terrance's front companies. This money traveled through several Swiss banks and one German. I traced it all the way back to its source at a holding company in—of all places—Langley, Virginia.

"I further found the original account was in fact a slush fund used jointly by the CIA and the Department of Homeland Security to pay off informants and lesser criminals in order to get the big ones.

"Any agent that makes use of this account needs to enter an access code to make a withdrawal. Even though I have the perpetrator's code, access to the owner's name is restricted beyond my abilities to find. I cross-referenced the appearance of the suspect code with all known assaults against federal agents, and I found a pattern. Each agent who was slain or brutally injured was paired up with other agents. I had a list of thirty-seven names. I took off all injured agents, and that left me with nine names. I then removed all the agents who were killed, and that left me with one name.

"Each time this code appeared, within a span of two weeks, agents were killed or hurt badly, just like Agent McFearson was years ago."

A crowd of two million people sat in stunned silence. Never before had any governmental agency been so fully exposed in real time, and the darkness George spoke about before was about to have a spotlight shown on it.

"This suspect was curiously absent," Phil continued, "during all the attacks. I also pulled all the financial records for this individual and discovered a vast fortune cleverly hidden among false retirement funds and investment companies."

As Phil spoke, the documentation that put him on the suspect's trail was scrolling over the monitors. The amounts totaled tens of millions of dollars.

"Terrance George was not the only criminal this person made use of. This person employed ten known drug lords. Three are still at large. Our suspect killed the rest." Phil concluded.

Every person present was holding his or her breath in anticipation of Phil's next remarks. From the end of the table, a shillelagh rocketed laterally across the top of the table. It rose up just enough to catch Agent Marlin squarely in the forehead, and it knocked him backward in his chair and to the ground. Dan threw his own chair aside, and he brought his shillelagh up over his head to strike the final blow on Dirk. Both Secret Service agents responded quickly, though. They wrestled Dan away from the fallen Agent Marlin.

"That piece of shite nearly had me killed. Twice!" Dan yelled.

As one agent held Dan at bay, the other cuffed a seriously disoriented Dirk and led him away.

George rose from his seat and walked over to Dan. He put a hand on his shoulder. "Dan, please calm yourself. There are more important matters to attend to at this time."

CHAPTER 31

Dan's anger subsided a bit, and as George and Dan were returning to their seats, President Saunders addressed Phil.

"Agent Hancock, please forward all your evidence to the Department of Homeland Security's director so it can be reviewed. Is there anything else?"

"Not at this time, Mr. President," Phil responded.

"Thank you, Agent Hancock. That will be all," Saunders concluded.

Phil's image disappeared, and the monitors returned to the normal television broadcast. Waves of murmurings washed over the assembled crowd.

"You assured me, Mr. Washington, you had irrefutable proof of your identity. I believe I'd like to see it now," the president said.

"Very well. I asked Agent McFearson to be present because he also doubts my claim. I have seen that he possesses remarkable integrity and a fervent desire to find the truth in all things. So I ask him to depart from here alone to my former home at Mount Vernon. Once there, he will enter my family tomb, and with the help of some others awaiting his arrival, he will open the sarcophagus that bears the inscription of my name. Should it hold remains, he is to retrieve the dental work and return with it for your inspection."

"There is a television news crew," Jeff interjected, "and a researcher, Dr. Samantha Snyder, already there. Dr. Snyder will retrieve the dental work for Agent McFearson and prepare it for transport. The news crew will film the proceedings so everyone can see there is no subterfuge at work here."

"I am not at all comfortable with opening a grave of such a distinguished historical figure," the president admitted. "However, I did give you my word to allow you to present your evidence. Agent McFearson, please go get Mr. Washington's evidence and return quickly."

"Aye, Mr. President. I'll be back in a jiffy," Dan stated as he departed.

Dan had only been gone a short time when President Saunders asked, "If you are who you claim to be, Mr. Washington, why didn't you just come forward to the authorities from the beginning?"

"I will yield that question to Mr. Thompson. Jeffery, if you please," George replied.

"President Saunders," Jeff began, "if an ordinary citizen came to the gates of the White House and asked to see you, that person would be turned away. True?"

Saunders replied, "Yes."

"If a person came up to the gates of the White House, asked to see you, and claimed to be *the* George Washington, that person would soon find himself or herself in a psych ward somewhere. True?"

Saunders hesitantly replied again. "Yes."

"Now, Mr. President," Jeff continued, "I want you to think very carefully about your answer to my next question. It only requires a yes or no. George and I have been straightforward and honest with you and your agents. We need you to be straightforward and honest with us and those behind us now." Jeff looked up into the air and shouted, "Isn't that right?"

The entire mass of people shouted together.

"Yeah! That's right!"

"Be straight with us!"

"Tell the truth!"

Jeff continued. "Are you ready for my question, Mr. President?" Saunders nodded. "If the authorities discovered a person was, in fact, some sort of time traveler, that person would have been apprehended and taken away to a secret facility somewhere. All knowledge of him or her would have been suppressed, and the public would have never known of his or her existence. Ever. Is that correct, Mr. President?"

President Saunders looked as though he was hoping for a well-timed asteroid strike to relieve him of the responsibility of answering. He looked at the vice president for some sign of support, but he was just as caught off guard.

It seemed like a century of awkward silence passed before George spoke. "President Saunders, I know the answer. I am cognizant of the discomfort of being put into a position in which one has to say something dreadful, even though it is the truth. If you can find the courage within yourself to speak the truth in this matter, then—at least as it pertains to me—you will still be worthy of the office you currently hold. You are not facing this moment alone, Mr. President. Your second-in-command is right there beside you, and more importantly, I am here. Please tell the truth, and then this conversation can move forward with ease."

The president steadied himself and tried to regain some lost composure. He looked George directly in the eyes and said, "Yes."

Massive waves of jeers flowed over the crowd. For the first time in US history, the president had told the truth about a controversial subject to the public. An air of hostility began to form from those in attendance.

George stood from his seat and walked to the podium that had been set up at the top of the Capitol building's steps.

"Citizens," George announced, "your attention please!" The ruckus of the crowd lowered, and George continued. "In the not-too-distant past, I cautioned you about being stirred to anger hastily. No good can come from condemning individuals before all the facts are known.

"I still believe this statement stands true. From the beginning of my journey until this very moment, President Saunders has acted honorably and with integrity. He has never deceived me to even the smallest degree, so far as I can recall.

"I would ask all present to consider this—do you know with absolute certainty I am who I claim to be? I could be a charlatan and a liar. Agent McFearson has not yet returned with the proof we all seek. So I ask all here not to be in haste. Let these events unfold as they will. The truth will be known this day."

Cheers went up, and George returned to his seat. President Saunders had a relieved expression when George returned.

CHAPTER 32

When Dan pulled into the parking lot he saw very few signs of life. A single vehicle sat with its headlights on at the service entrance. As Dan drove slowly toward the car, a man got out and approached his car. Dan turned his car so the stranger arrived on the driver's side. As the man got closer, Dan put his hand under his jacket and gripped his gun tightly.

When the stranger was close enough, Dan said, "Hold it right there, fella. Who are you?"

"I am John Langdon, the curator," the man stated. "I'm here to escort you to the tomb. I was told you would be here, Agent McFearson. Shall we go? The others are waiting."

"Lead on, sonny boy," Dan asserted.

Mr. Langdon got back in his car and drove across the estate to the tomb with Dan in tow.

Once the introductions were made, Dan said, "Listen up, people! I'm the agent in charge of the mission, so you'll all be followin' my orders. This is not gonna be a media circus. Only Dr. Snyder, Mr. Langdon, and I will be goin' into the tomb. The news crew will get what coverage they can from outside as we enter and leave. If your view angle be discreet enough, you can film the artifacts being removed from the coffin. At no time will you film the body itself. Are ye understandin' me, folk?"

A chorus of "yes, sirs" was heard, so Mr. Langdon unlocked the iron gate, and the three-person crew entered. The cameraperson was down on one knee, shooting nearly level with the top of the sarcophagus. The reporter was describing the action in great detail.

Mr. Langdon applied a flat metal pry bar to the area between the lid and the box. After a few moments, there was a discernible pop as the lid lost its grip. Dan and Mr. Langdon slid the lid at the head of the sarcophagus to the side—just enough to allow Dr. Snyder to view the contents.

Dr. Snyder put a small box with foam padding on the inside on the lid. She put on a pair of surgical gloves and a mask and began to examine the coffin's contents.

The two men stood back to give the doctor room to work. Dan continued to watch the news crew for any signs of impropriety, but so far everyone was cooperating.

Dr. Snyder announced, "OK, gentlemen. Here we go."

Very carefully, she reached down and grasped what looked to be the lower portion of a dental device. She pulled it from the coffin and set it inside the safety box. She repeated her motions and retrieved the upper portion as well.

Dan and Mr. Langdon placed the lid back squarely on the coffin and then exited the tomb with the doctor. Mr. Langdon locked the iron gate again. Then Dan interrupted the news reporter.

"You and your crew, follow me and the doctor. Keep filmin' as we go. We're not home free until we get to the president. Let's move."

The news crew van fell in behind them as they recrossed the estate and left the grounds. Even though there were two million people standing in the Mall, the traffic on the way back to the Capitol building seemed light. Plus it appeared as though all the traffic lights they encountered turned green as they approached. Dan found it curious until he realized what was going on. Then he smiled slightly to himself. The car pulled into the reserved parking area, and four Secret Service agents met them. Dan and Dr. Snyder were escorted to where the president sat.

"Well, Dr. Snyder, how do we proceed?" Saunders asked.

"It's very simple, Mr. President," Dr. Snyder claimed. "I'll set the samples we just collected before you, and with this magnifying glass, you can compare them with the samples George is going to give you. You don't need a degree in advanced medicine to do a straight comparison. On the monitors you've seen us collect these specimens and the direct trip here. These are your control items. If George's differ in any way, he is not who he claims to be. Are you ready, Mr. President?"

"Proceed," Saunders said, and he gulped.

The doctor helped the president with his surgical mask and a pair of gloves. Then she laid a white linen towel in front of the president. She opened the safety box and carefully set both dental pieces on the cloth. She changed gloves and walked to the opposite side of the table. George removed his teeth and handed them to Sam. George could tell she was smiling at him under her mask. She returned to the president and placed them before him, as well.

Saunders asked, "May I have one cameraperson come closer to the table as I review this evidence?"

George agreed, and the cameraperson who had filmed the tomb was brought forward to document the comparison.

The magnifying glass was placed on a stand in front of the president, and with a lower piece in each hand, he viewed the details of each part in turn. After a few minutes, he repeated the process with the upper dental work.

Jeff was watching on a monitor as the president studied the lower denture, and he noticed something that sent a wave of fear through his body. He shook it off for the time being, but from then on, his observations were foremost in his thoughts.

The president finished his comparison, placed the recovered artifacts back in the safety box, and handed George's teeth back to Sam. Sam made her way back to George. Standing there beside him was Clara with a bowl of antiseptic wash for George to clean his teeth in.

Once George put his teeth in their proper place, he asked President Saunders, "Mr. President, what are your conclusions?"

President Saunders looked at George for a few moments. Then he and the vice president stood and walked to George's side of the table. George stood as Saunders approached, and then Saunders stopped in front of George, extended a hand, and said in a commanding tone, "Welcome back, President Washington. You've been gone for a very long time."

Cheers and all manners of good tidings enveloped the crowd. The adulation continued until George asked Saunders if he might address the citizens again. The president escorted George to the podium, and George raised a hand. The audience's fervor began to subside.

CHAPTER 33

"Citizens of the United States, harken unto my words. Pay heed to what I have to say!

"I am George Washington, first president of these United States and one of the Founding Fathers of this country. I am cognizant of the fact that history records my death over two hundred years ago. My appearance in these modern times would seem impossible. I do not understand the forces that have allowed me to be here at this place and this time, but perhaps understanding is not necessary.

"There are many assembled here who accept my identity on faith. I thank you for your open minds and hearts. There are even more of you who are here and viewing this assembly in your homes who doubt my identity and believe me a charlatan and a liar.

"To the doubters I owe a very large debt of gratitude. They doubt and seek to discern truth in given matters. They are the ones who find the courage to ask the most powerful question ever exchanged betwixt two people—why?

"Why does the federal government seem to have forgotten the citizens who created it and whom it serves?

"Why do the members of Congress subject the citizens to health care they themselves do not participate in?

"Why do the members of Congress make careers of their offices? That is not the way it was intended.

"Why do the members of Congress vote for their own pay raises? The citizens are not afforded that ability.

"I can stand here and cite many more questions concerning the decline of this institution that I and others have worked so hard and sacrificed so much to create, but I also have questions I would like to pose to the general population.

"Why have you allowed this government to subjugate you so unjustly?

"Why are the polls increasingly devoid of voters each year?

"Why have you not taken back that which was taken from you? This is the right of accountability.

"I have studied the history that has transpired since this country's founding, and what I have seen vexes me to my core. One evening's debate will not resolve all the nation's evils. One rousing speech will not dispel the apathy that has become so prevalent among its citizens.

"I call upon every citizen of this country to shake off the pacification that has been a way of life for so long. Choose to make a daily effort to involve yourselves in the affairs of state. Otherwise, this republic will not stand the test of time and will be subject to the decay that has been the fall of every major civilization since the beginning.

"Mr. Thompson and I have spent many long hours putting into words possibilities and ideas that, with your help, will strengthen our nation and increase the accountability of the government to its people.

"Be ready, citizens of the United States of America, for change is on the horizon, and your hands will bring it—as it should be."

More applause could be heard resounding off the buildings and monuments of the Mall. George stepped aside, and the president took the podium. Once the applause decreased, he spoke.

"My fellow Americans, we are in the midst of extraordinary events this evening. Through unknown means, the very first president of this nation has returned to us. From what I can gather after speaking with him, he is not at all pleased by how the country has fared since he founded it.

"I now declare President Washington is under the protection of the Secret Service. He has all the rights and privileges granted former leaders of this country.

"We will continue to investigate the cause of his arrival, and a full disclosure of the investigation's progress will be made to this nation's people so the stigma of the black ops nature of this government can begin to be eliminated.

"Make no mistake, there are national security issues to be dealt with, so there will never be a time when the government is completely transparent, but every governmental branch can do better at being accountable to you, the citizens.

"I will listen to President Washington's and Mr. Thompson's ideas carefully, and if I find their suppositions are based in logic and reason, then I will put them before you, the voters, to accept or reject. President Washington is correct. There is change on the horizon, and the time for this country's citizens to take a more active role in its continuation is at hand."

The four architects of this evening's event stood together at the top of the Capitol building's steps and waved to all the people who had helped George regain the presidential stature he had once had. Even though there was uncertainty in the future, at least the cornerstone of a foundation for positive change had been laid.

CHAPTER 34

Two million people made their way back home. Perhaps for the first time in their lives, they didn't feel as though the government was a foe that could not be vanquished.

The hour was late, and Clara had taken her leave of George for the evening. She was escorted to a guest room in the White House to sleep. George, Jeff, and President Saunders sat in a private sitting room and reflected on the day's events.

After a pause in the conversation, George said, "President Saunders—"

The president interrupted. "We are not in the public view anymore. Please call me Darius. First names are more agreeable to me."

"Very well then, Darius," George continued. "There is one matter I wish to resolve before I retire for the evening. I would like Jeff and me to go to my home at Mount Vernon. I have a need to see some more familiar surroundings and dispel these anxious feelings I have been plagued with since my entrance into the modern age. I shall return before the morning comes."

"As a former president, you are at liberty to come and go as you please. I ask you to take some Secret Service with you just in case, though," Darius suggested.

"Sound counsel. Thank you, Darius," George said gratefully.

Before long, Jeff, George, and a Secret Service agent were pulling up to the front door of the manor house at Mount Vernon. The curator was waiting for them. George asked the curator and Secret Service agent to remain at the entrance while he and Jeff explored the house for a while.

The first room Jeff and George visited was the large dining room. Colonial period chairs and furnishings stood around the perimeter, and on the mantel of a huge fireplace was an object George knew very well. It was the sword John Bailey had made for him in Fishkill, New York. John had immigrated to the United States from Sheffield, England, some years before. He was a master sword smith who had caught George's attention at the beginning of the revolution. As a hanger sword, it was forged of steel with a grooved blade. Green-dyed ivory composed the grip. It had a silver strip to adorn the handle, as well. To complete the weapon, Mr.

Bailey had fashioned a leather scabbard with silver trim to contain the instrument he had worked so hard to create.

George was admiring his battle sword as it sat upon the stand when Jeff said hesitantly, "Uh…George, there's something I think you should know."

"What is it?" George replied.

"When President Saunders was comparing your teeth to the ones recovered from the tomb, I noticed the lower piece from the tomb had the same three small blue dots as yours—the ones put there when Sam took the samples to study."

"What are you trying to say, Jeffery?" George asked.

"Sam put those dots there in the future. In order for your teeth to end up in the coffin in your family tomb, you have to return to your home in the past. The dots were faded, and I think I was the only one to notice, but they were there. That means at some future time, you'll be going back home."

The gravity of Jeff's observations and deductions unsettled George. He had just spent a considerable amount of time and effort to make a new life for himself here, and yet he couldn't help but feel elated at seeing his friends and family once again. What about Clara, though? She would be left alone yet again. After the adventures she had shared with him, would she ever be satisfied with simply going back to work at the library?

George had a pensive expression when he said, "I have no words to describe the flood of thoughts I am grappling with at this moment. Let us continue our journey through these halls as I contemplate the full meaning of your words. Perhaps at its conclusion an epiphany will be found."

As the pair wandered from room to room, George shared stories of his life in this house. In the kitchen, he remarked on a time when he was a young boy and one of the female slaves who had worked in the kitchen was showing him some meal preparations. For several hours, he helped her get the dinner ready. When his father came in and saw George laboring, George was given a severe spanking, and the woman was sent to work in the fields from then on.

George made it clear he had good times and fond memories of his time on his father's estate, but tobacco production and the presence of slaves overshadowed much of it.

In an upstairs bedroom was a mannequin who was wearing some of the everyday clothes George had worn back in the day. Jeff found it amazing they were nearly identical to the clothes George had been wearing the morning they met on the beach.

Jeff had an interesting idea. "Say, George, let's do something kind of fun. How's about you put on this set of ordinary clothes, and I'll take a picture of you posing like a mannequin right here beside a mannequin. I bet you Clara would get a big laugh from such a picture."

"That does sound rather fun, Jeffery," George admitted. "But would it be appropriate? After all, this is a museum."

"George," Jeff said, "these are your clothes, are they not?"

"They are indeed." George agreed.

"I'll go back out to the car and grab my camera. I'll be back by the time you're done changing," Jeff said.

Jeff left the room and headed for the entry door at the far side of the house. George took the clothes off the mannequin and put them on. Even though the material was two centuries old, it still felt warm and familiar, and it brought a measure of peace to George's troubled thoughts.

CHAPTER 35

Jeff went down the stairs and through three rooms to get to the foyer. Because there were only a few lights on, he couldn't see some areas of the house. Jeff expected to find the curator and the Secret Service agent inside the door conversing quietly, but as he approached the open door, they were not there. Jeff looked around the room but could find no sign of them.

Since the door was still open, he thought maybe they had gone outside, so he stepped out on the front porch. To his horror, he saw the agent and Mr. Langdon lying in a large pool of blood at the bottom of the steps. Jeff turned and ran back into the house. As he crossed the threshold, something collided with the back of his head, and he fell to the floor, unconscious.

George had put his two-hundred-year-old street clothes on and was admiring himself in a mirror. He was gratified that Iustitia looked equally as handsome with his common clothes as it did with his uniform.

Fifteen minutes had passed, and Jeff had not returned. George returned to the entryway to see what was keeping him. When he entered the room on the far side, he could see the door standing open and Jeff's body lying on the floor.

Iustitia was immediately called upon, and George moved quickly to Jeff's side. He put his hand near Jeff's mouth and found he was still breathing. George stood and gazed around the darkened room. There were many shadows that could conceal a person, and then he realized who had attacked his friend.

George said in a commanding voice, "Agent Marlin, show yourself. Or do you prefer slinking about the shadows like the dog you are?"

Dirk stepped forward into the dim illumination at the center of the room. Dirk was dressed in light-gauge body armor from toe to head. He wore a riot helmet with a face shield, and protective padding covered his forearms, thighs, and shins.

"I see your tailor has provided you clothing suitable to the profession of a jester," George jabbed. "It would seem the Secret Service is not as formidable as I first assumed."

"Apparently," Dirk stated, "the old saying that if you want something done right, you should do it yourself is in full force here. I gave King George two chances to get you, and he blew it twice. Even after all the time and trouble it took me to bust him out of the hospital.

"Washington, you have cost me a vast fortune, and for that I am going to make sure you stay dead this time," Dirk growled.

"'Tis indeed unfortunate," George said, "you have chosen this course of action. In the words of today's urban youth, let us rock!"

Dirk was wielding a marine corps KA-BAR knife, and as he circled George, Dirk said snidely, "You always favored your homemade weapon. It only uses blunt force in battle, and you will find my jester's clothes are well suited to stop your Iustitia."

George lunged forward with a blow from the side. Dirk blocked it with his forearm and countered with a back slash of his knife. This opened a small wound on George's right bicep. George recoiled and moved forward again, but before he reached striking range again, Dirk dropped to the floor and used his leg to sweep George's out from underneath him. As he fell, the knife came up from the floor and laid open his right thigh.

George was lying on his back and bleeding when Dirk launched himself through the air. With both hands on the hilt of his knife, he was going to plunge it deep into George's chest as he landed.

Fortune favored George, though. As Dirk was making his descent, George brought his left leg up and caught Dirk in the sternum with his boot. With a mighty thrust, George used Dirk's own momentum to hurl him back over George's head. Dirk was helpless as he sailed through the air and out the still-open door. His velocity was such that he cleared the porch altogether and landed at the foot of the steps on the bodies of the two men he had killed.

George didn't linger long on the floor. Even though he was bleeding, he managed to right himself and gather his strength. Dirk entered the door a moment later and started to charge across the room at George.

Dirk was halfway across the room when George heard someone shout his name. From his peripheral vision, he saw something flying through the air toward him.

George switched Iustitia to his left hand, and with his right he caught the grip of a familiar sword. With Iustitia in one hand and his battle sword in the other, George turned the tide of battle to his favor. Dirk was upon him an instant later. George dipped his right shoulder down and then brought up his forearm, so Dirk's straight charge turned into a glancing blow.

George recovered to the center of the room and announced to Dirk, "You will never see the sunrise again!"

George began to walk slowly toward Dirk. Again, George's ballet-like fencing movements began to pick up speed, and when Dirk met him, Iustitia came up from the side and crashed a blow to the side of his helmet. Then the sword came down on Dirk's arm between the armored segments at his elbow. It left a gash in the material. George spun clockwise and unleashed Iustitia on the other side of Dirk's helmet and yet another slash to the armor's binding material.

Like the work of an expert marksman, each blow to the helmet disoriented Dirk momentarily, and that gave George the opening to cut the armor apart at its weakest points. Dirk tried to back away, but George kept up the advance. Finally, George had him backed against a wall. Dirk knew he was losing. In an act of desperation, he withdrew a pistol and brought it up to bear on George. An instant before Dirk pulled the trigger, George crammed Iustitia's little brass ball down the barrel. When the round discharged, the gun blew up in Dirk's hand and took the greater portion of that hand with it.

George took what was left of Iustitia and swung it upward. He caught the bottom of Dirk's face shield. This kicked his head back and his chin up, and George used the last of his strength to thrust his sword upward under Dirk's chin, through his skull, and into the wall behind him.

George was exhausted, and he began to fall backward. Before he hit the floor, though, Jeff was there to catch him. After a few moments, Jeff and George moved to sit on the floor with their backs on the wall that still had Dirk's body pinned to it.

After a period of silence, Jeff asked, "How badly are you hurt?"

"'Tis a bit more than a scratch, but I shall live to fight another day," George replied.

"I think both of us should avoid fighting altogether. We are getting far too old for this amount of stress. You especially," Jeff said.

"I am inclined to agree with you at this juncture. I am feeling my age upon me," George said wearily.

Jeff helped George out to the car and administered a field dressing to George's leg.

The two men sat in the front of the car and stared out the windshield. All they had just witnessed transfixed them.

Without breaking his gaze, George said, "When the opportunity presents itself, I will be returning to the past. 'Tis where I belong."

"Yeah, I kind of thought you would," Jeff said sadly. "I know you have been missing your friends and Martha, but just so you know, when you do leave, you will be missed terribly."

"I am curious to know when my departure will be," George said quietly.

"Have you considered going to the spot in the woods where this whole thing began? That would be a good place to start."

"What about the bodies littering the estate? Should we not attend to them?" George asked.

"I don't think they are in a hurry to go anywhere. Besides, you are more important at the moment," Jeff said. "There are roads all over this estate. Just point in the right direction, and we'll see where they lead."

George and Jeff drove down the access roads to the estate's southern end. There weren't a lot of woods left, but George said the marshy area was on the southern end on the ocean side of the property, so they headed in that general direction.

They approached the tree line and sat there for a few minutes. They watched and were unsure what to do next.

George said it had been completely dark the night he left, so Jeff shut the car off. The men sat in the dark and listened.

CHAPTER 36

A half hour passed, and Jeff was about ready to call it. The sun was going to come up in about an hour, anyway. George tapped Jeff on the arm and pointed at an area of the woods. Sure enough, there was a small amount of light glowing through the trees.

The pair exited the vehicle and slowly made their way through the brush. In a matter of minutes, the two men were standing within twenty yards of the light. It was on the ground just as George had described in the beginning. Ribbons of color were emanating from the ground and stretching up into the sky. The luminous area was about fifteen feet in diameter, and it carried a reasonably bright aura.

"Well, George, I think your ride is here," Jeff whispered.

"Indeed, Jeffery. It would seem so," George replied.

"I have a very hard time saying good-bye, George, so I will simply thank you for your friendship and for giving me a purpose so now I can make a difference," Jeff said sincerely.

"You have been my good right arm through all the trials this journey has taken us on. I fear I would have been incarcerated somewhere dreadful if you had not come to my aid. You will be missed as well, and please give Clara my best. Good-bye, Jeffery."

With that, George walked toward the area of illumination. He stood at its edge for a few minutes, and then the light flared brightly. After it dissipated, the light and George were gone.

The sun was peeking over the horizon when Jeff made it back to the car. He phoned the authorities and met them back at the house. There was a lot of explaining to do.

Sometime later and back in Washington, Jeff stopped by the Library of Congress and looked up George's obituary. It said George died on the same day he had originally, but this time it was from complications of a leg wound he had suffered while returning home through the woods that night. Everyone around him had no knowledge of George's initial cause of death. This was most likely from some shift in the timeline. Jeff never confirmed it, but he thought his proximity to George and the event portal might have spared his memory from any changes.

Even though the past was pretty much the same as it always had been, the future would certainly unfold differently now. George's influence changed the way the citizens regarded the government, and the politicians in Washington were given very little choice but to change to better suit the people.

George had once said, "This nation can and will be great once again."

Jeff believed him.

ACKNOWLEDGMENTS

I'd like to thank the staff of the Stanley Hotel of Estes Park, Colorado, for providing me a wonderful atmosphere conducive to inspirational writing.

ABOUT THE AUTHOR

R. W. Belew, Sr., has had a lifelong interest in the sciences—particularly time travel—which led him to pursue a career as a robotics technician. His daily interaction with technology and fascination with the issue of causality provide the basis for *New Beginnings*, as well as for future books in the series.

Belew once said, "Causality is something not to be trifled with," which he proves to be true through his stories. Belew believes there's not one person alive who hasn't wanted to go back in time to change their fortunes, but there is an infinite set of possible outcomes if even the smallest event is altered.

The biggest question Belew's readers will have is "What if?" Possibilities are endless when dealing with time.

R. W. Belew Sr. is considered to be a deep thinker and much time is spent considering many scenarios for each action contained in *New Beginnings*.

Made in the USA
Charleston, SC
28 January 2016